BEYOND THE WESTERN DEEP

STORY BY ALEX KAIN ART BY RACHEL BENNETT

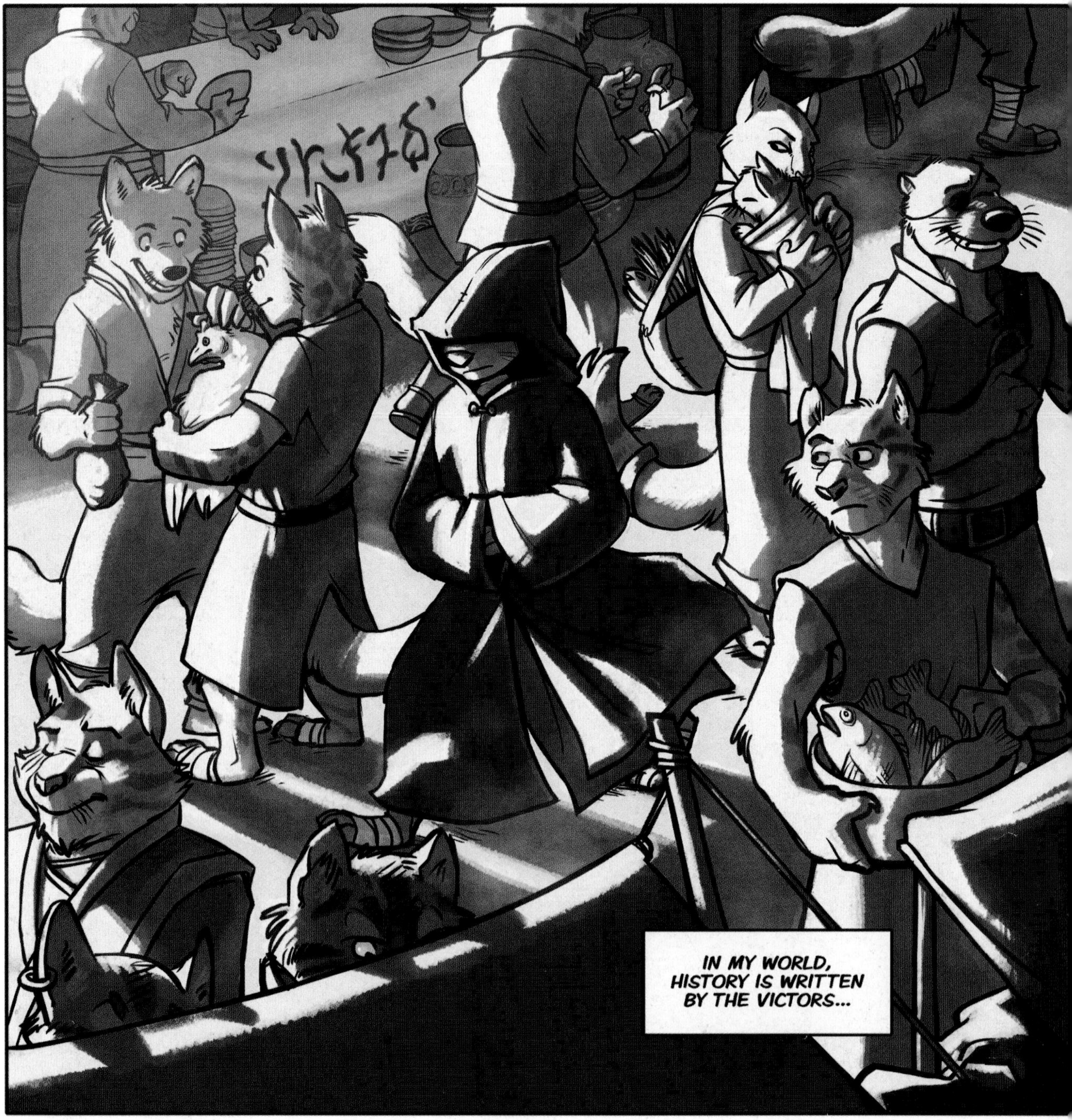
IN MY WORLD, HISTORY IS WRITTEN BY THE VICTORS...

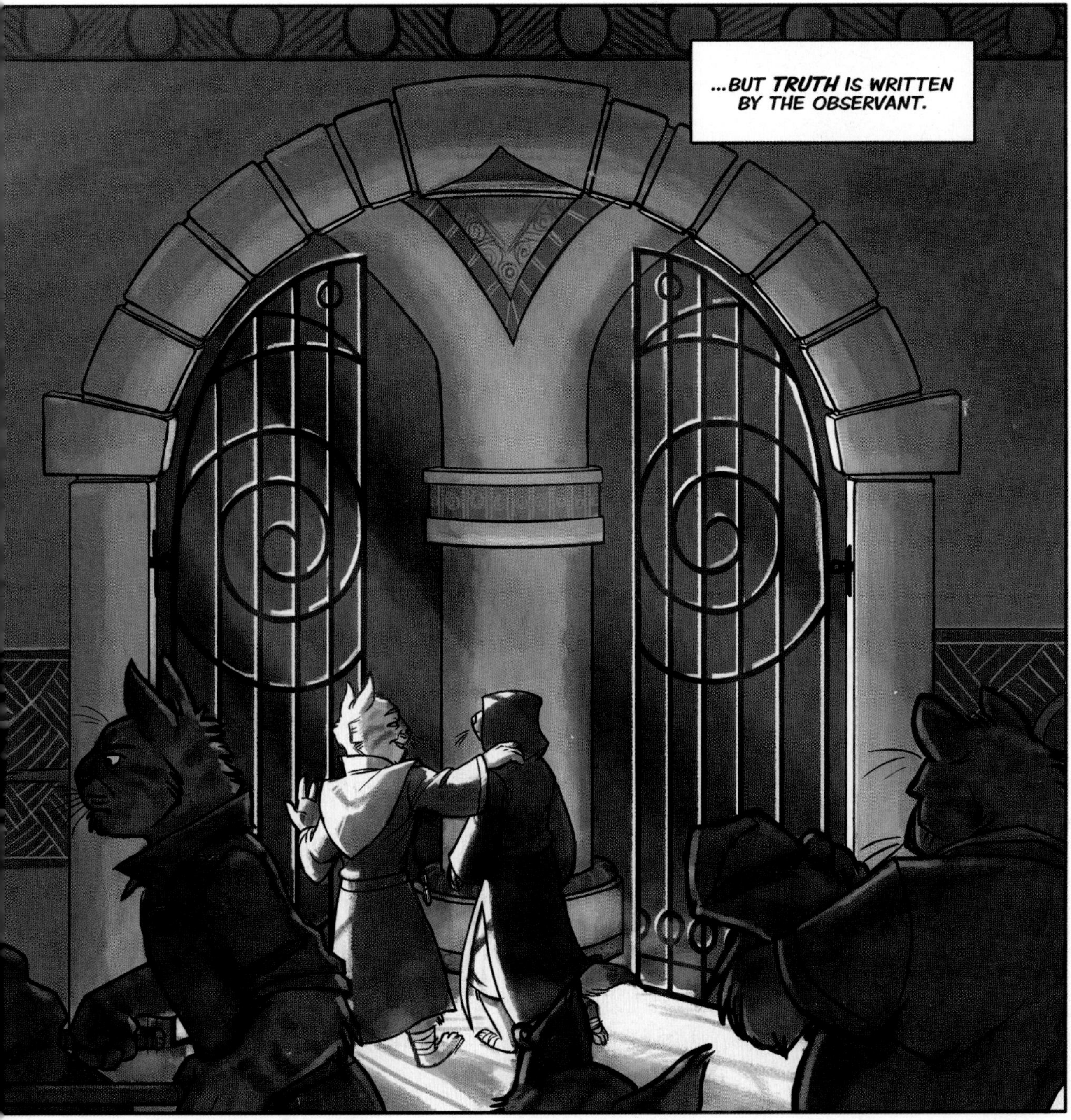
...BUT *TRUTH* IS WRITTEN BY THE OBSERVANT.

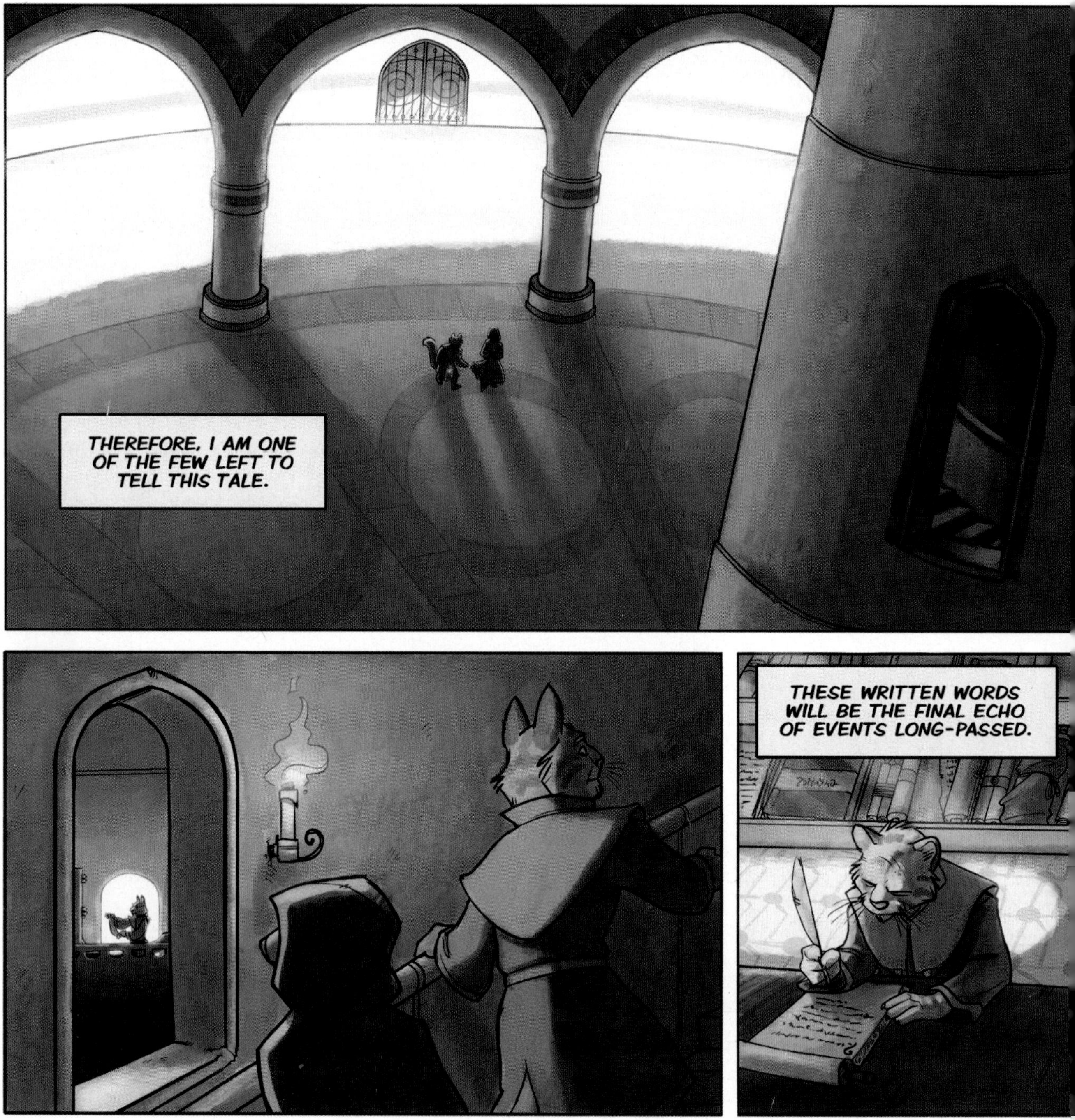
THEREFORE, I AM ONE OF THE FEW LEFT TO TELL THIS TALE.
THESE WRITTEN WORDS WILL BE THE FINAL ECHO OF EVENTS LONG-PASSED.

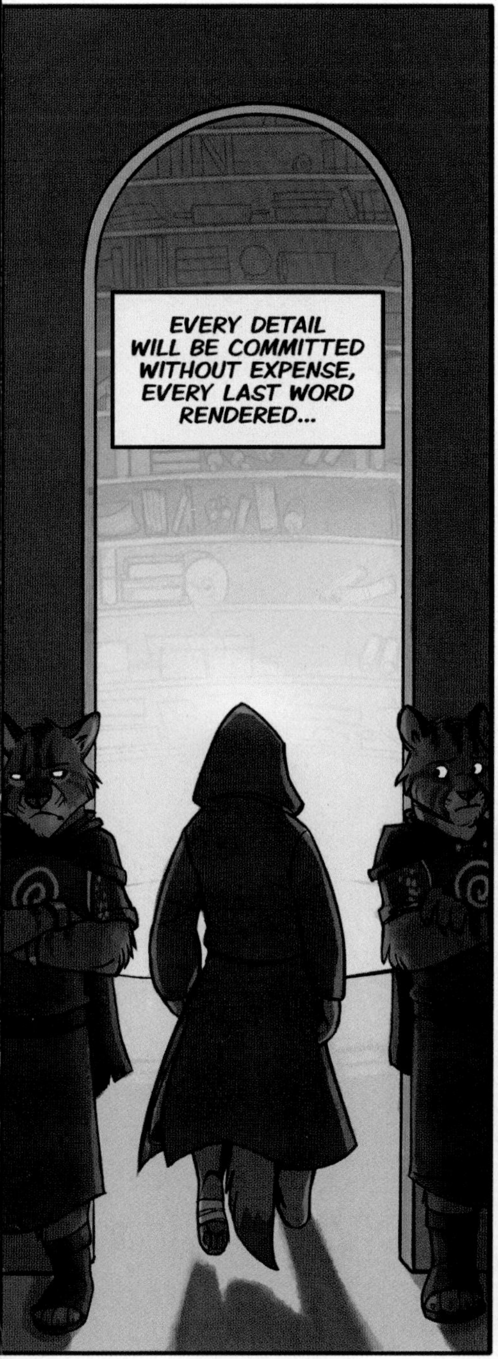
EVERY DETAIL WILL BE COMMITTED WITHOUT EXPENSE, EVERY LAST WORD RENDERED...

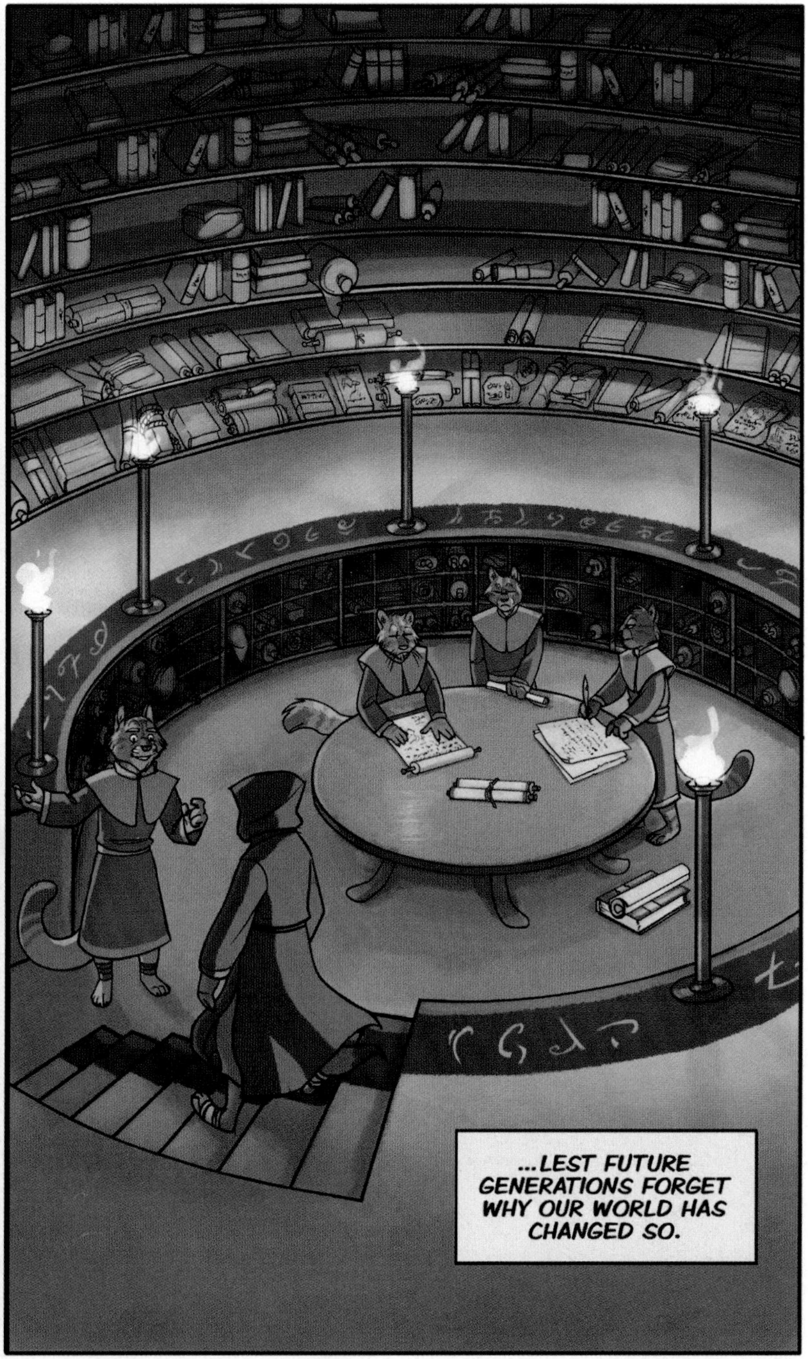
...LEST FUTURE GENERATIONS FORGET WHY OUR WORLD HAS CHANGED SO.

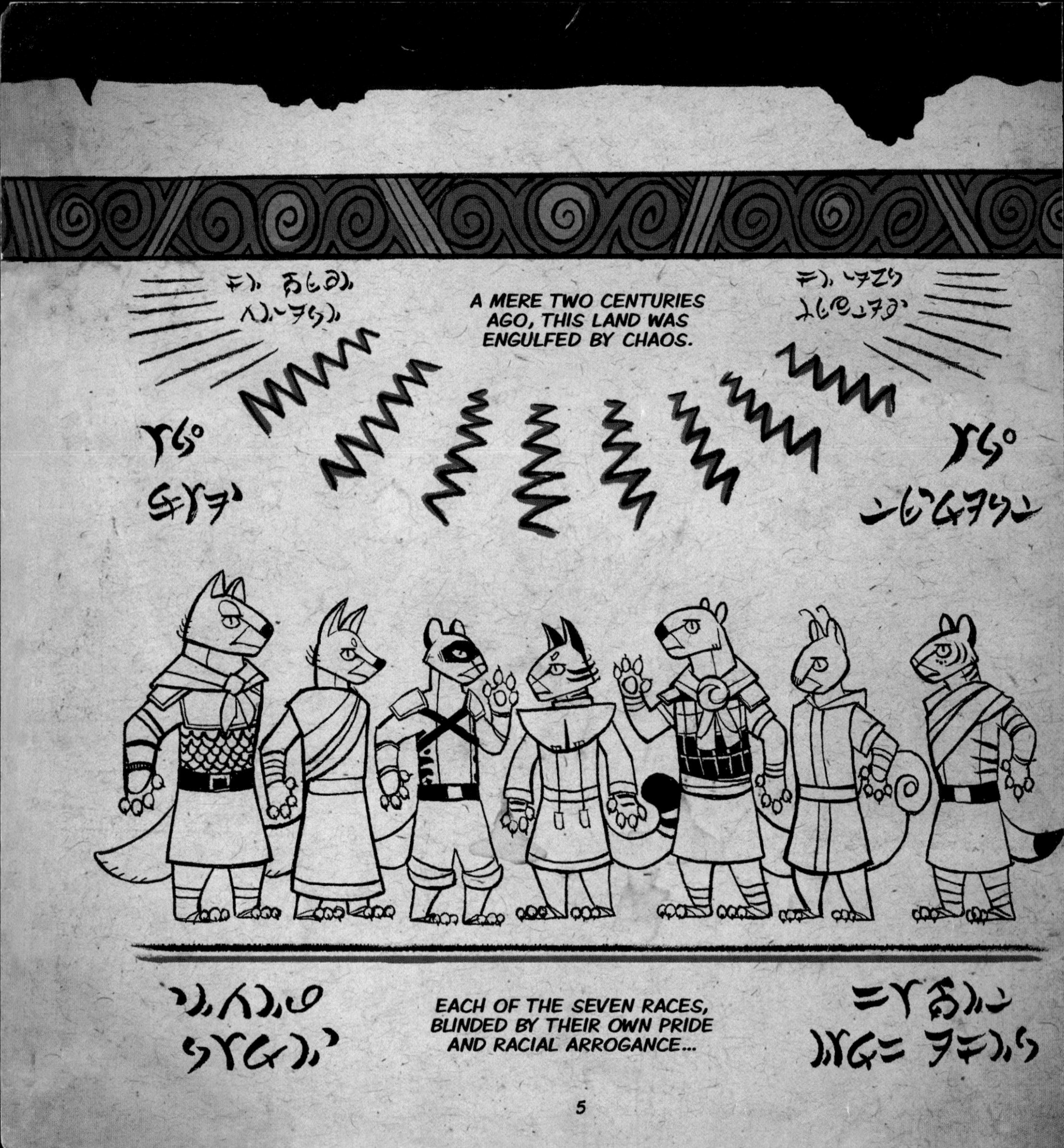
A MERE TWO CENTURIES AGO, THIS LAND WAS ENGULFED BY CHAOS.
EACH OF THE SEVEN RACES, BLINDED BY THEIR OWN PRIDE AND RACIAL ARROGANCE...

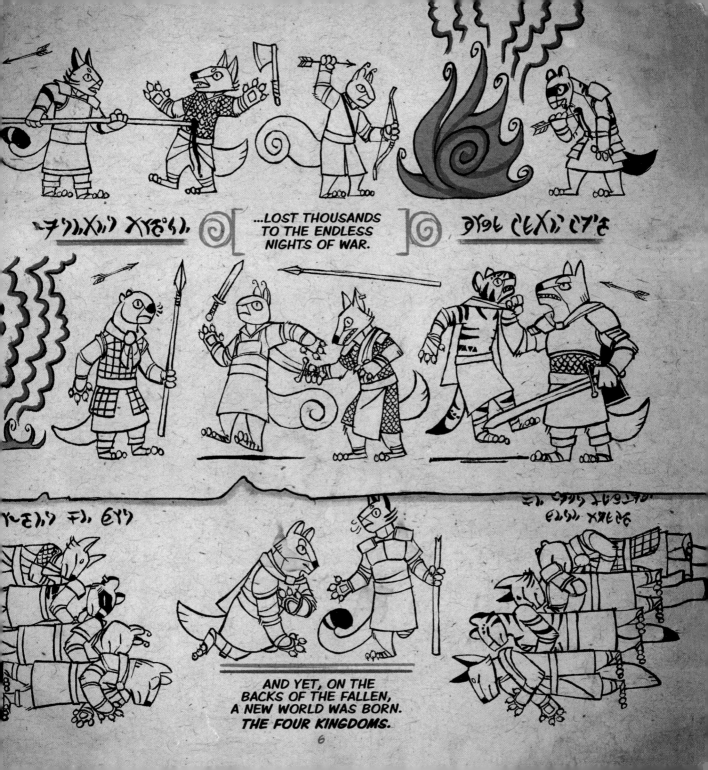

...LOST THOUSANDS TO THE ENDLESS NIGHTS OF WAR.

AND YET, ON THE BACKS OF THE FALLEN, A NEW WORLD WAS BORN. *THE FOUR KINGDOMS.*

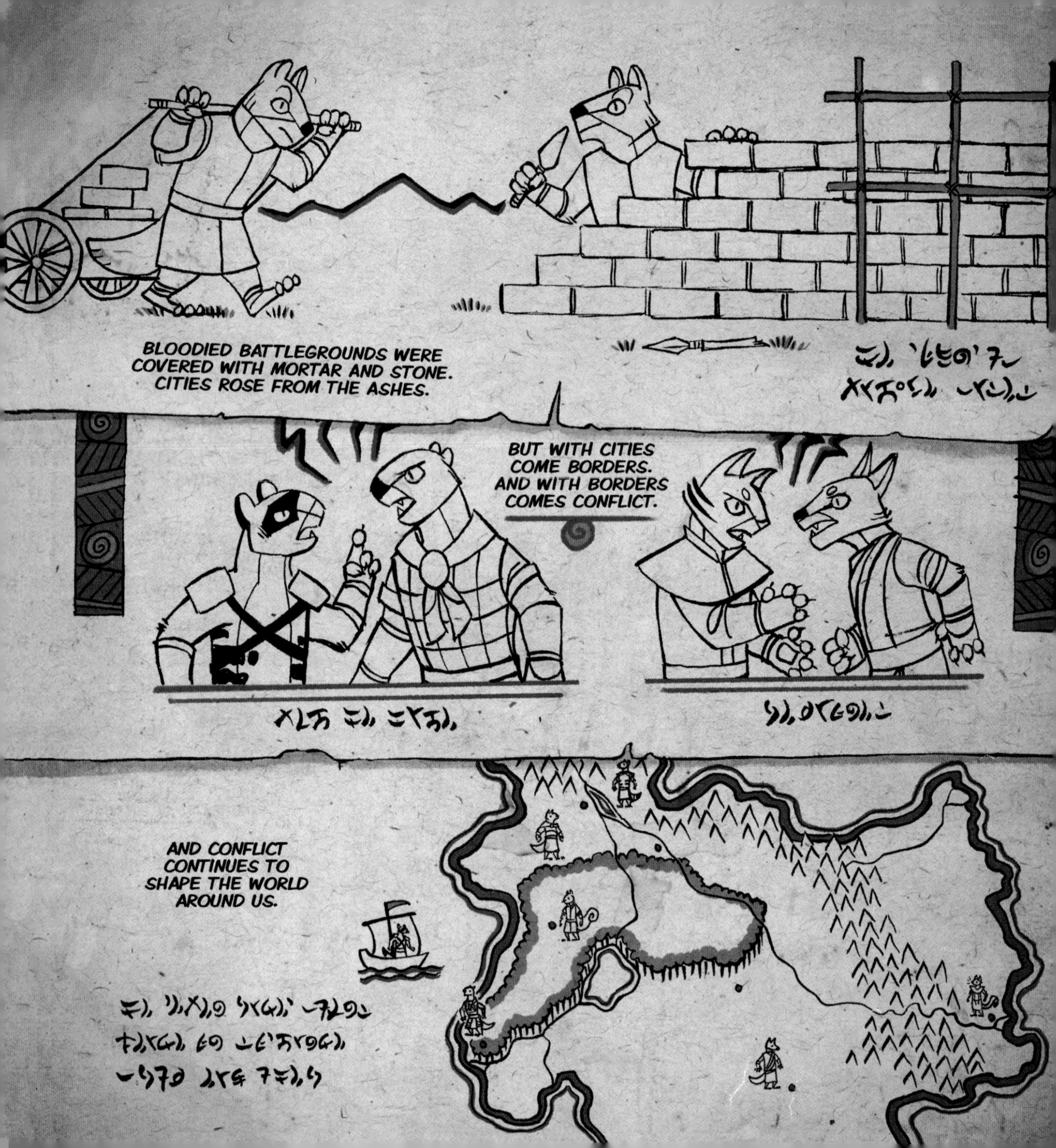
BLOODIED BATTLEGROUNDS WERE COVERED WITH MORTAR AND STONE. CITIES ROSE FROM THE ASHES.
BUT WITH CITIES COME BORDERS. AND WITH BORDERS COMES CONFLICT.
AND CONFLICT CONTINUES TO SHAPE THE WORLD AROUND US.

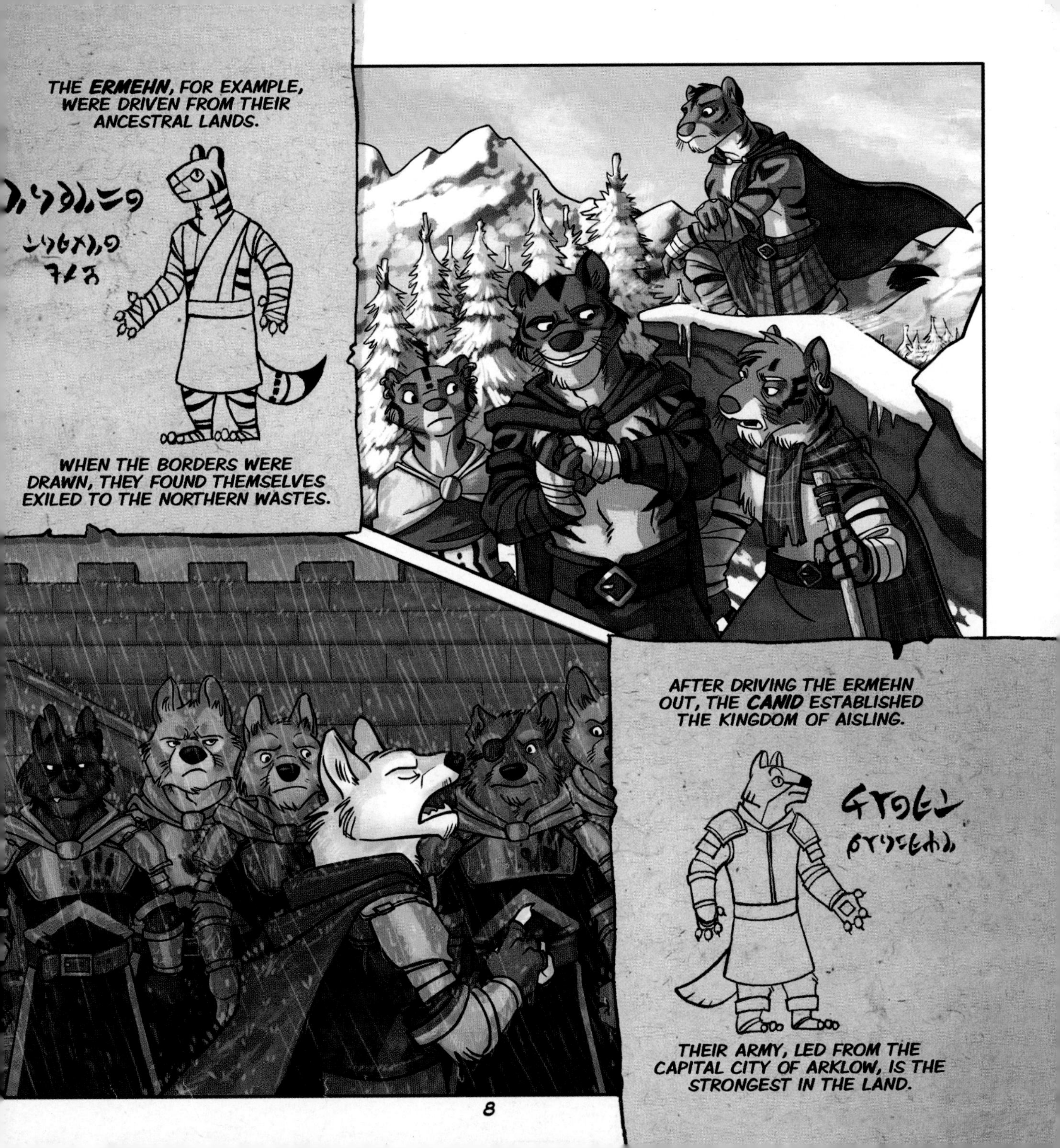
THE ERMEHN, FOR EXAMPLE, WERE DRIVEN FROM THEIR ANCESTRAL LANDS.
WHEN THE BORDERS WERE DRAWN, THEY FOUND THEMSELVES EXILED TO THE NORTHERN WASTES.
AFTER DRIVING THE ERMEHN OUT, THE CANID ESTABLISHED THE KINGDOM OF AISLING.
THEIR ARMY, LED FROM THE CAPITAL CITY OF ARKLOW, IS THE STRONGEST IN THE LAND.

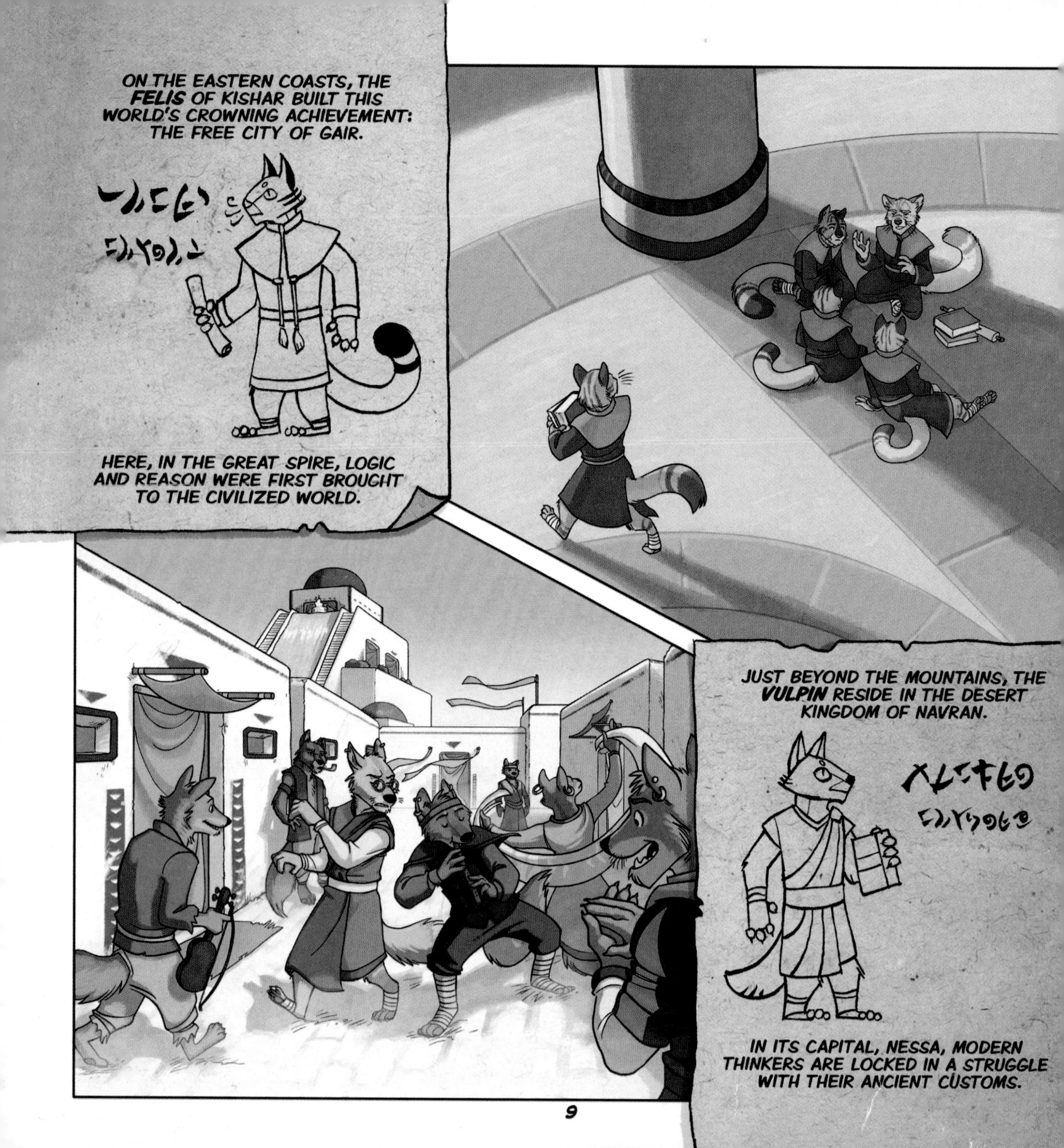
ON THE EASTERN COASTS, THE FELIS OF KISHAR BUILT THIS WORLD'S CROWNING ACHIEVEMENT: THE FREE CITY OF GAIR.
HERE, IN THE GREAT SPIRE, LOGIC AND REASON WERE FIRST BROUGHT TO THE CIVILIZED WORLD.
JUST BEYOND THE MOUNTAINS, THE VULPIN RESIDE IN THE DESERT KINGDOM OF NAVRAN.
IN ITS CAPITAL, NESSA, MODERN THINKERS ARE LOCKED IN A STRUGGLE WITH THEIR ANCIENT CUSTOMS.

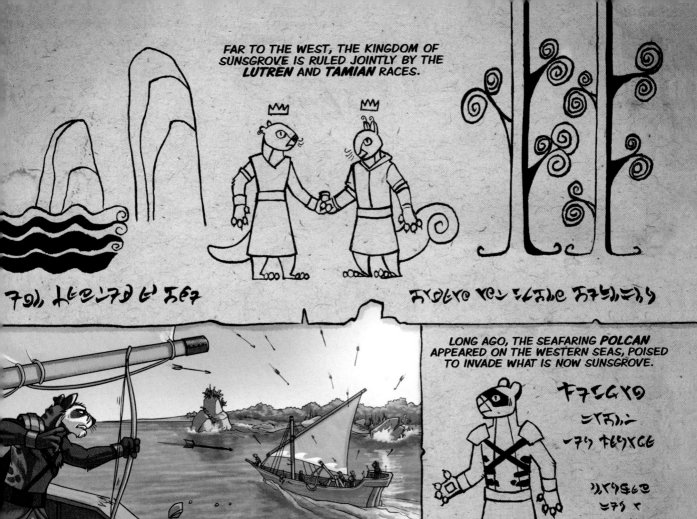

FAR TO THE WEST, THE KINGDOM OF SUNSGROVE IS RULED JOINTLY BY THE *LUTREN* AND *TAMIAN* RACES.

LONG AGO, THE SEAFARING *POLCAN* APPEARED ON THE WESTERN SEAS, POISED TO INVADE WHAT IS NOW SUNSGROVE.

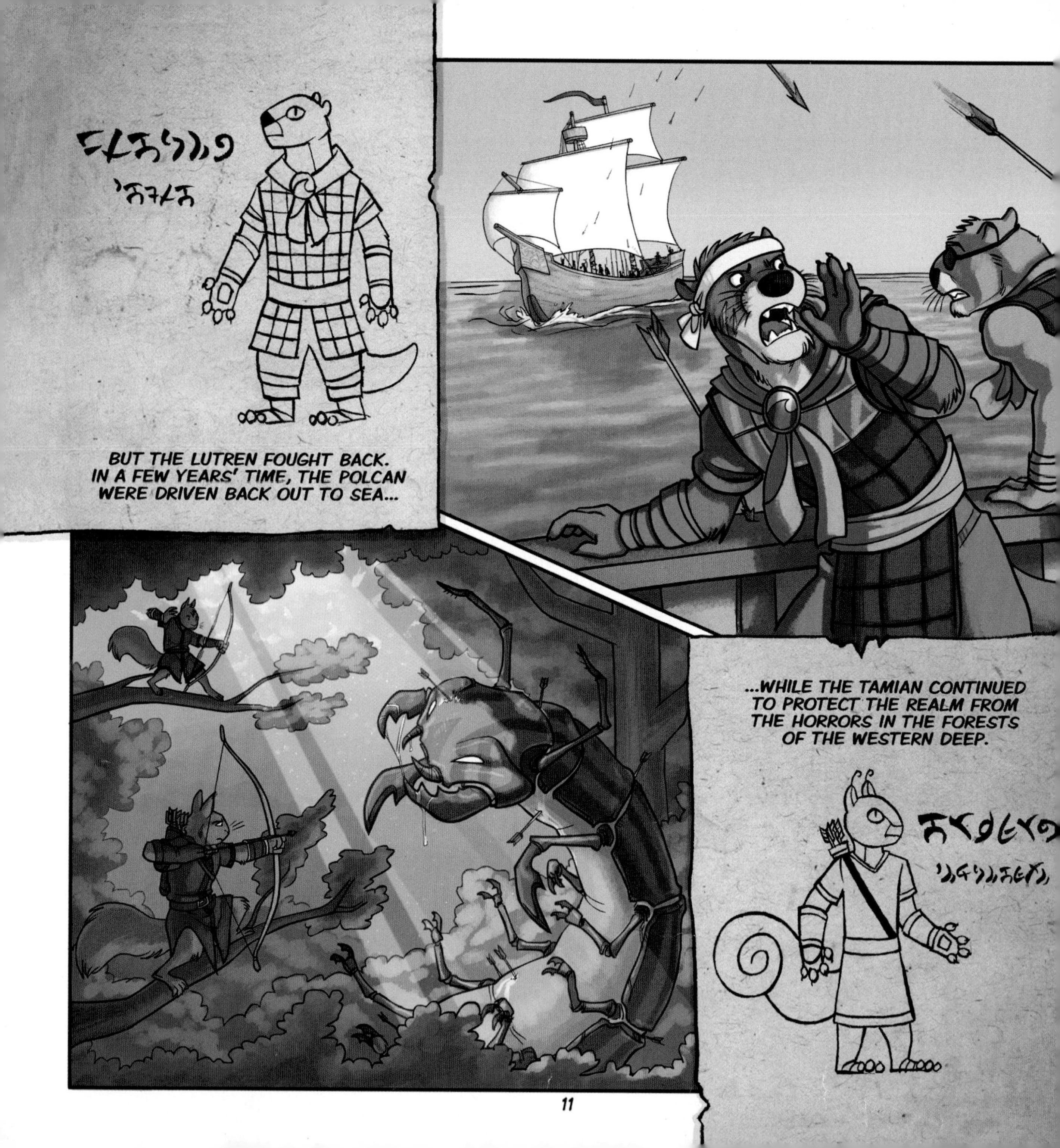
BUT THE LUTREN FOUGHT BACK. IN A FEW YEARS' TIME, THE POLCAN WERE DRIVEN BACK OUT TO SEA...
...WHILE THE TAMIAN CONTINUED TO PROTECT THE REALM FROM THE HORRORS IN THE FORESTS OF THE WESTERN DEEP.

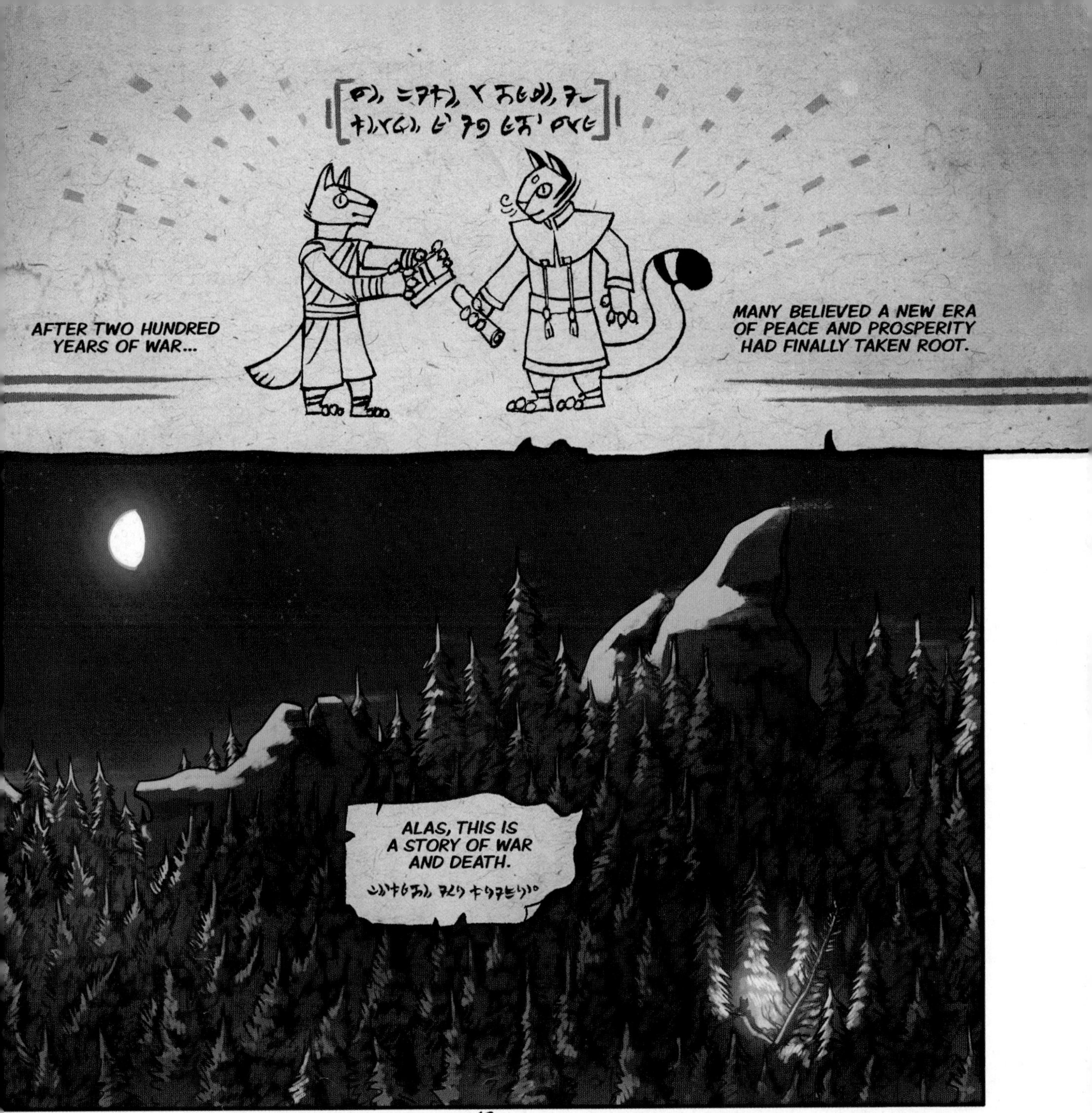
AFTER TWO HUNDRED YEARS OF WAR...
MANY BELIEVED A NEW ERA OF PEACE AND PROSPERITY HAD FINALLY TAKEN ROOT.
ALAS, THIS IS A STORY OF WAR AND DEATH.

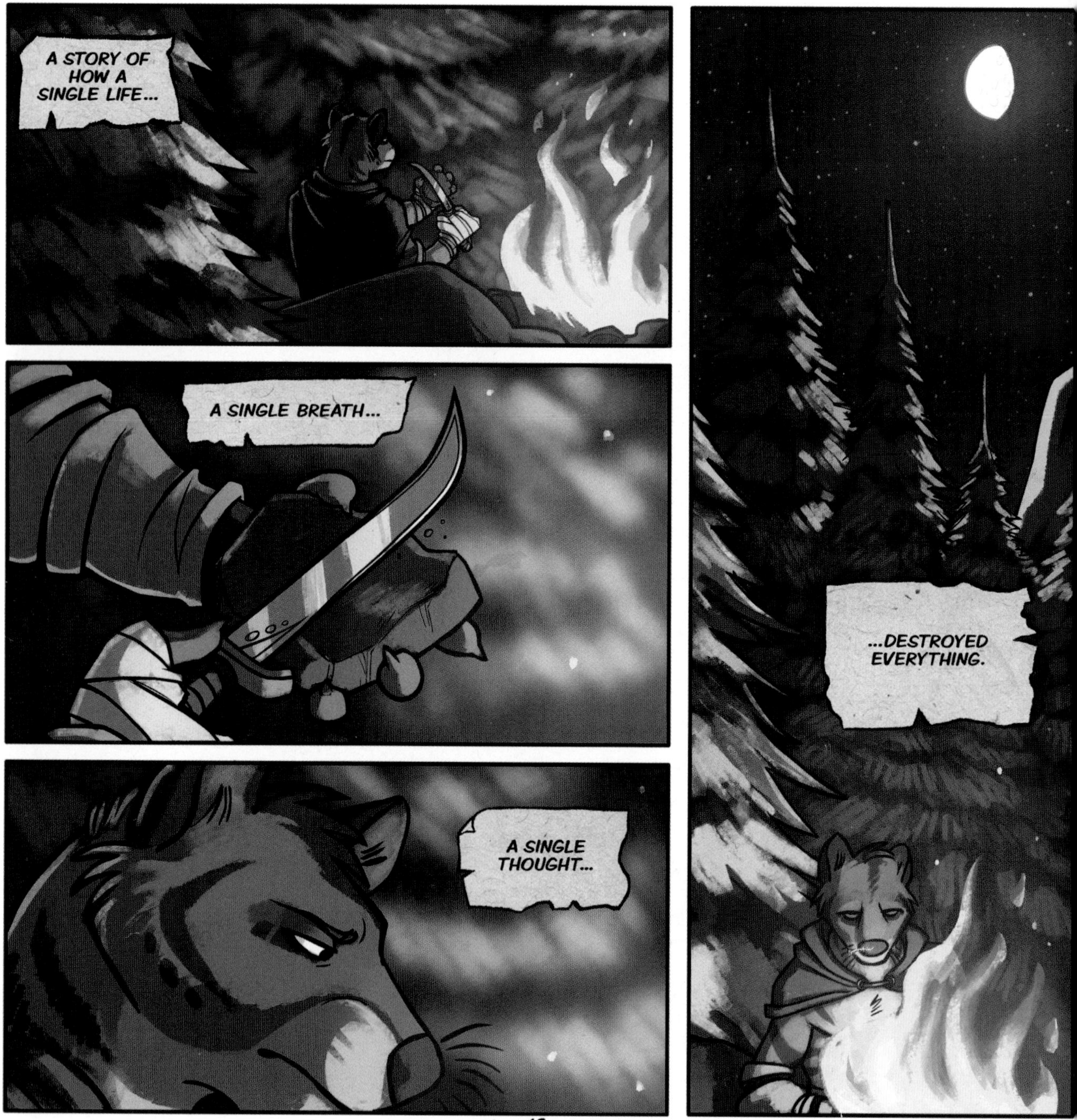
A STORY OF HOW A SINGLE LIFE...
A SINGLE BREATH...
A SINGLE THOUGHT...
...DESTROYED EVERYTHING.

CHAPTER ◈ ONE

THE FORESTS OF
THE WESTERN DEEP

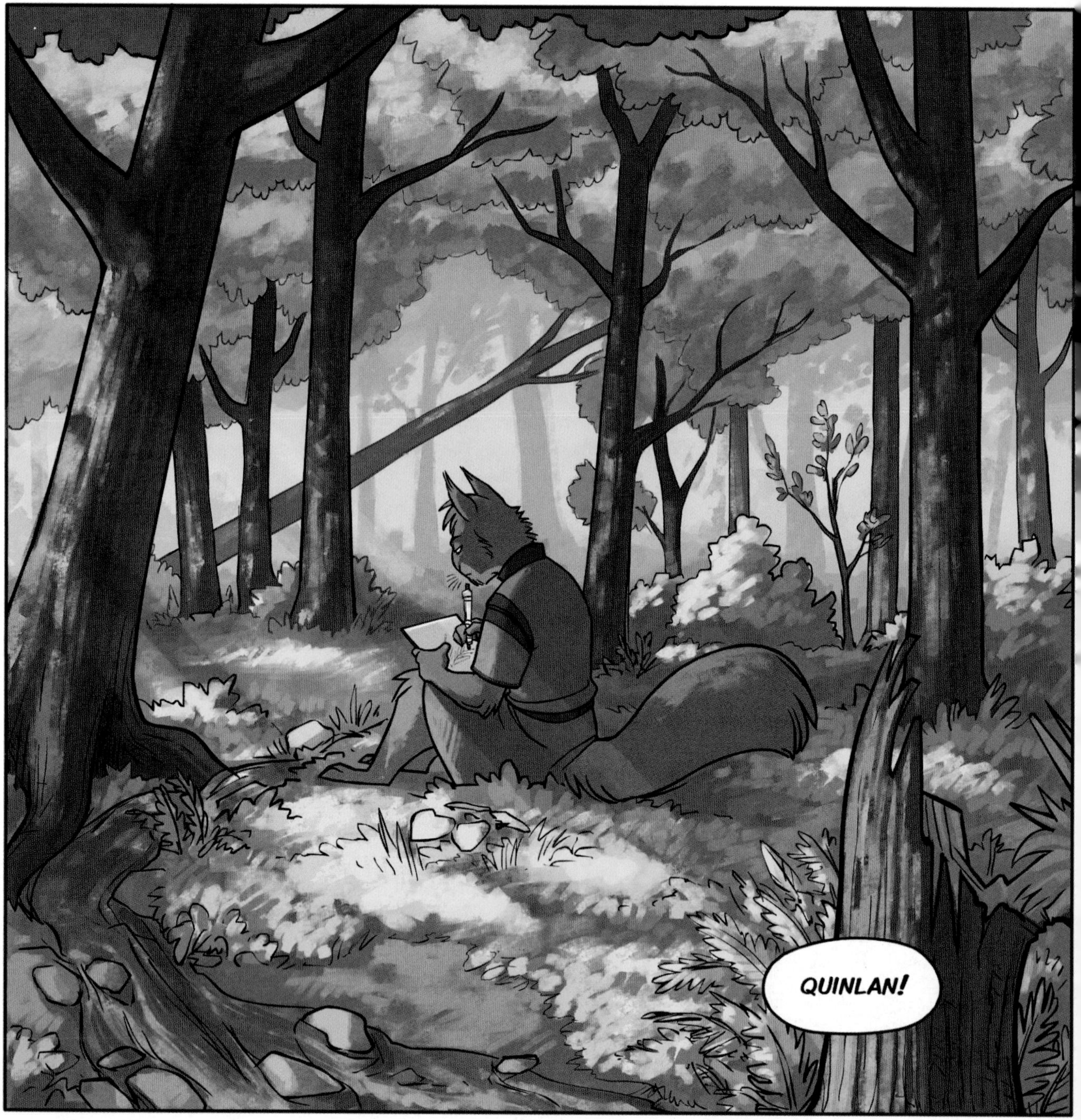
QUINLAN!

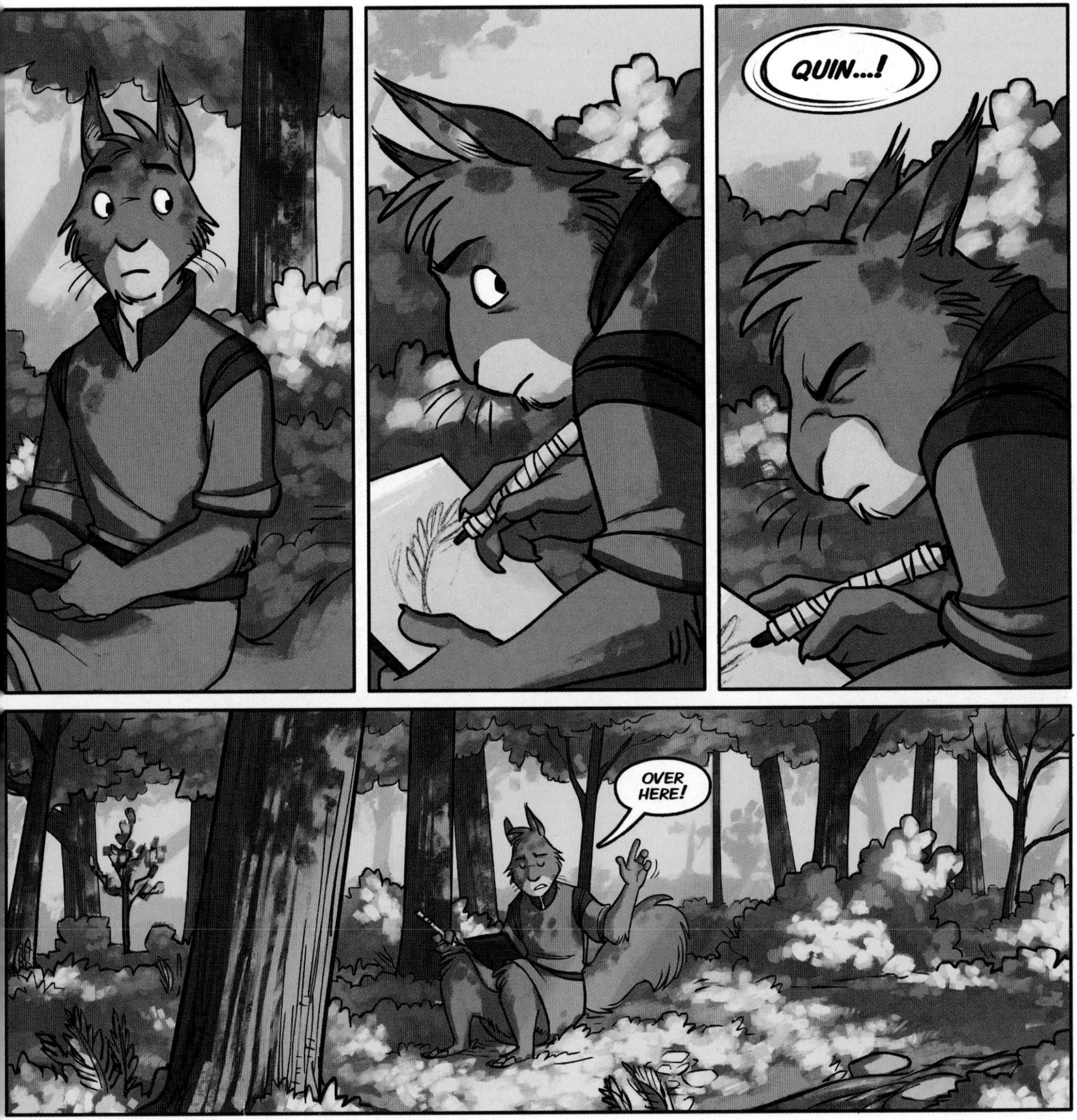
QUIN...!
OVER HERE!

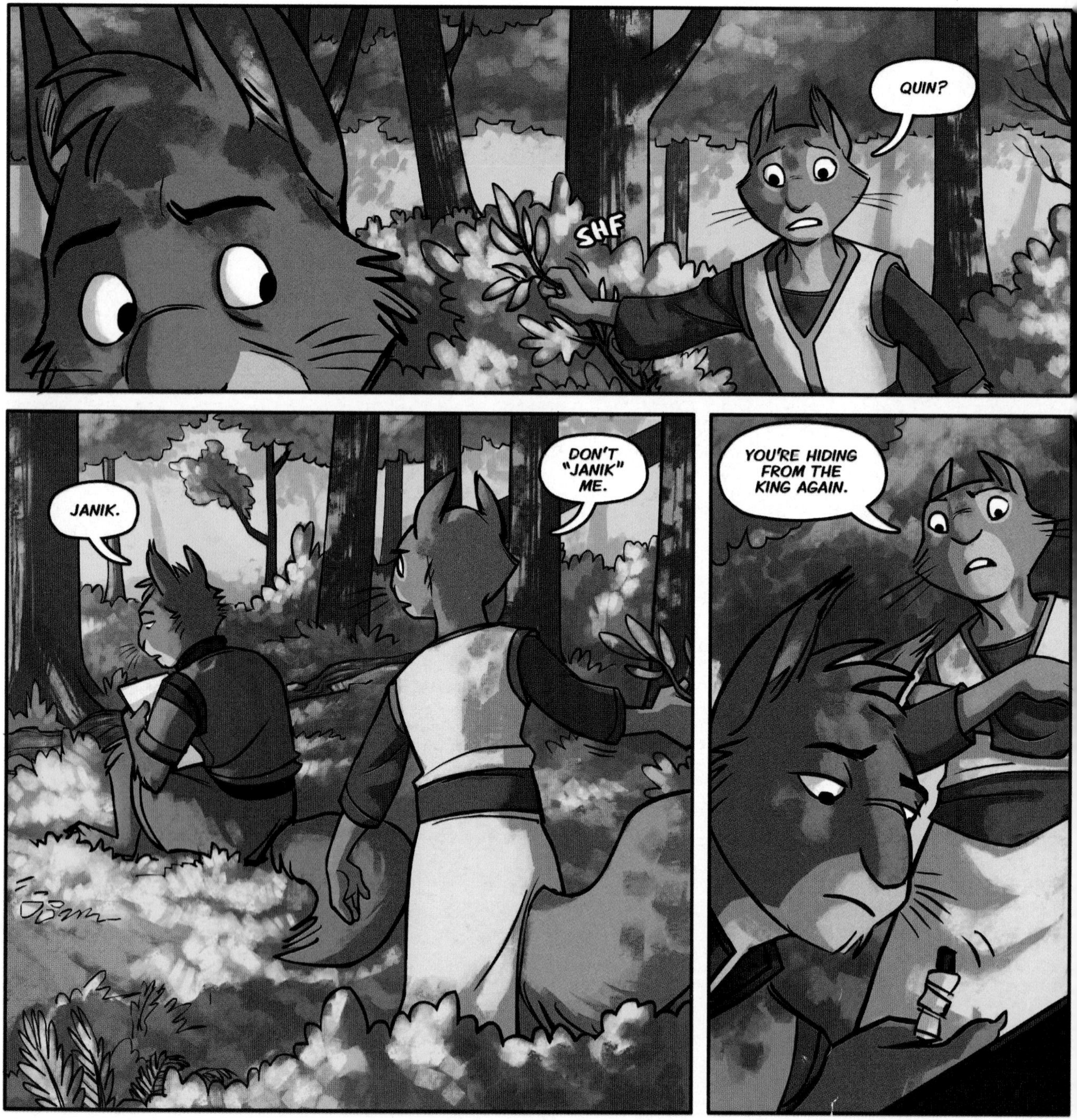

QUIN?
SHF
JANIK.
DON'T "JANIK" ME.
YOU'RE HIDING FROM THE KING AGAIN.

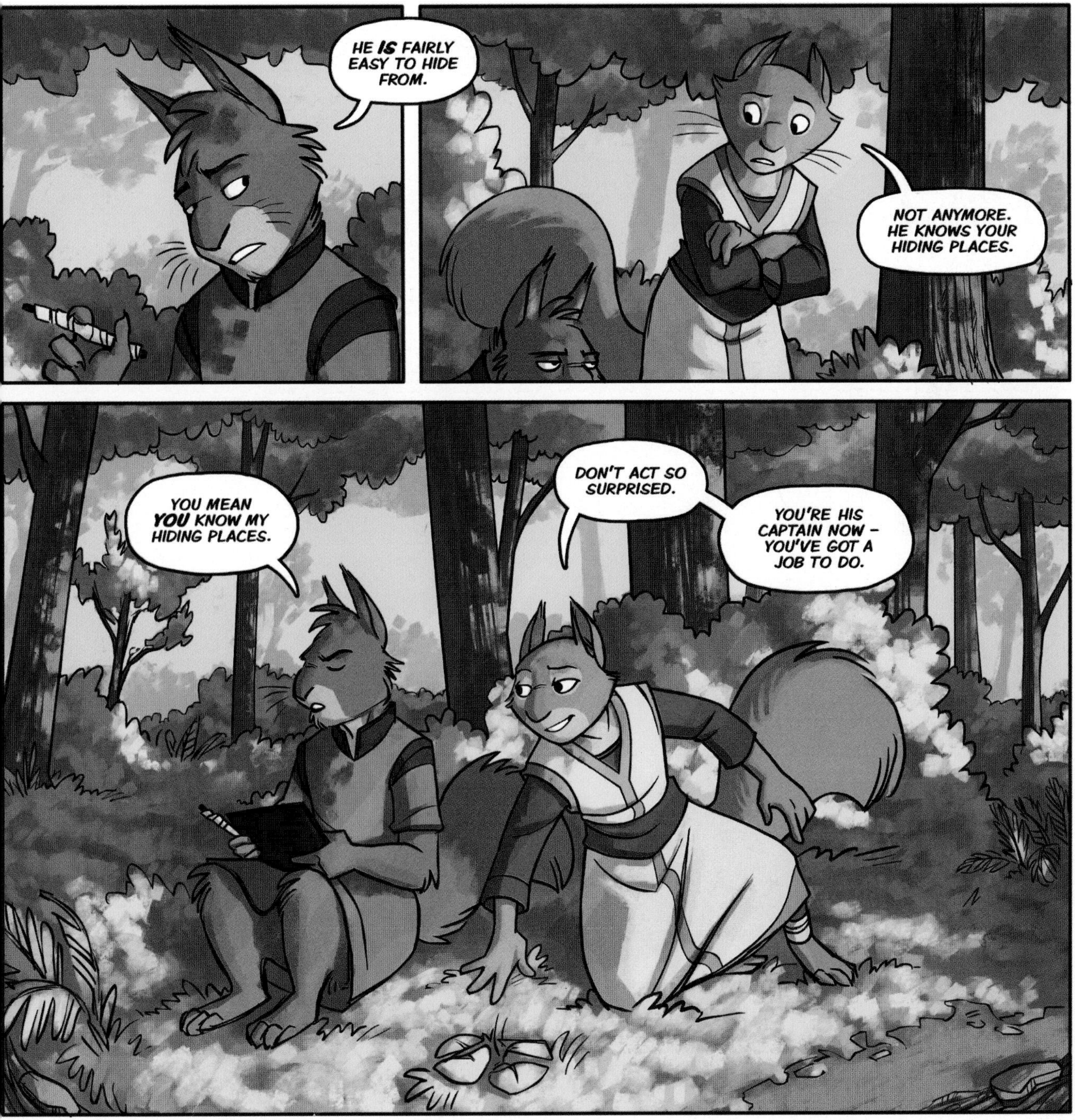
HE **IS** FAIRLY EASY TO HIDE FROM.
NOT ANYMORE. HE KNOWS YOUR HIDING PLACES.
YOU MEAN **YOU** KNOW MY HIDING PLACES.
DON'T ACT SO SURPRISED.
YOU'RE HIS CAPTAIN NOW - YOU'VE GOT A JOB TO DO.

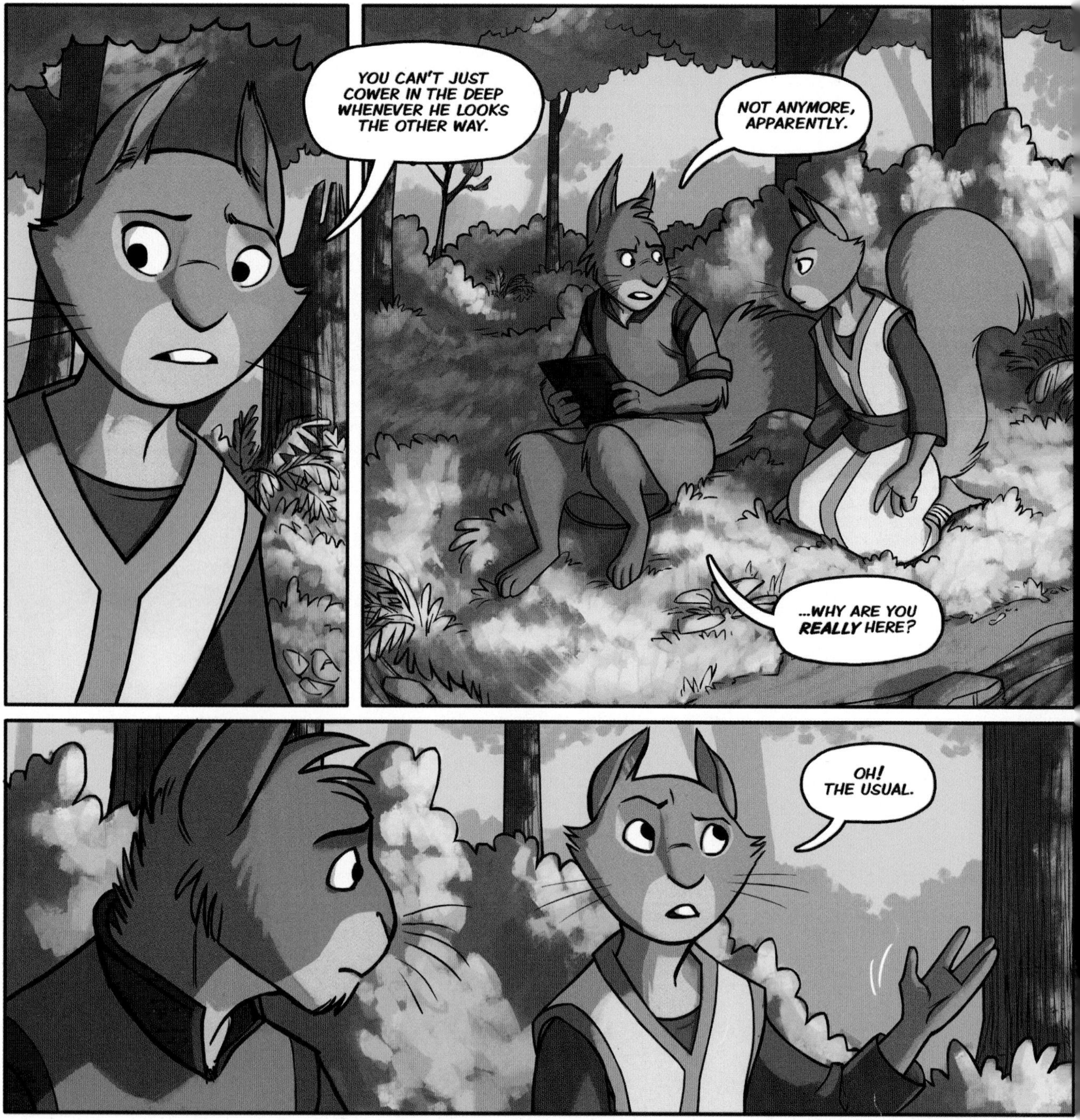
YOU CAN'T JUST COWER IN THE DEEP WHENEVER HE LOOKS THE OTHER WAY.
NOT ANYMORE, APPARENTLY.
...WHY ARE YOU *REALLY* HERE?
OH! THE USUAL.

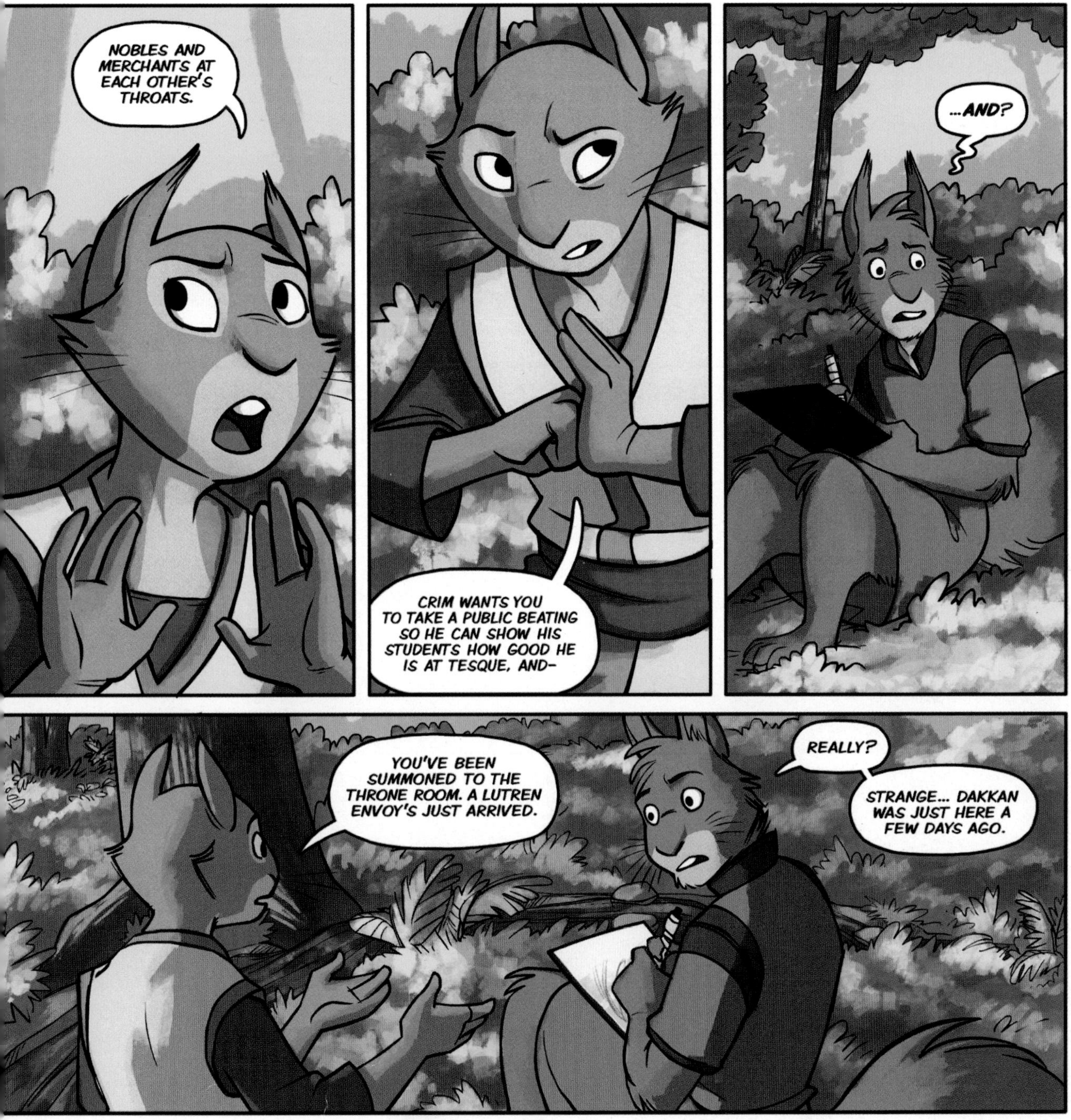
NOBLES AND MERCHANTS AT EACH OTHER'S THROATS.
CRIM WANTS YOU TO TAKE A PUBLIC BEATING SO HE CAN SHOW HIS STUDENTS HOW GOOD HE IS AT TESQUE, AND-
...AND?
YOU'VE BEEN SUMMONED TO THE THRONE ROOM. A LUTREN ENVOY'S JUST ARRIVED.
REALLY?
STRANGE... DAKKAN WAS JUST HERE A FEW DAYS AGO.

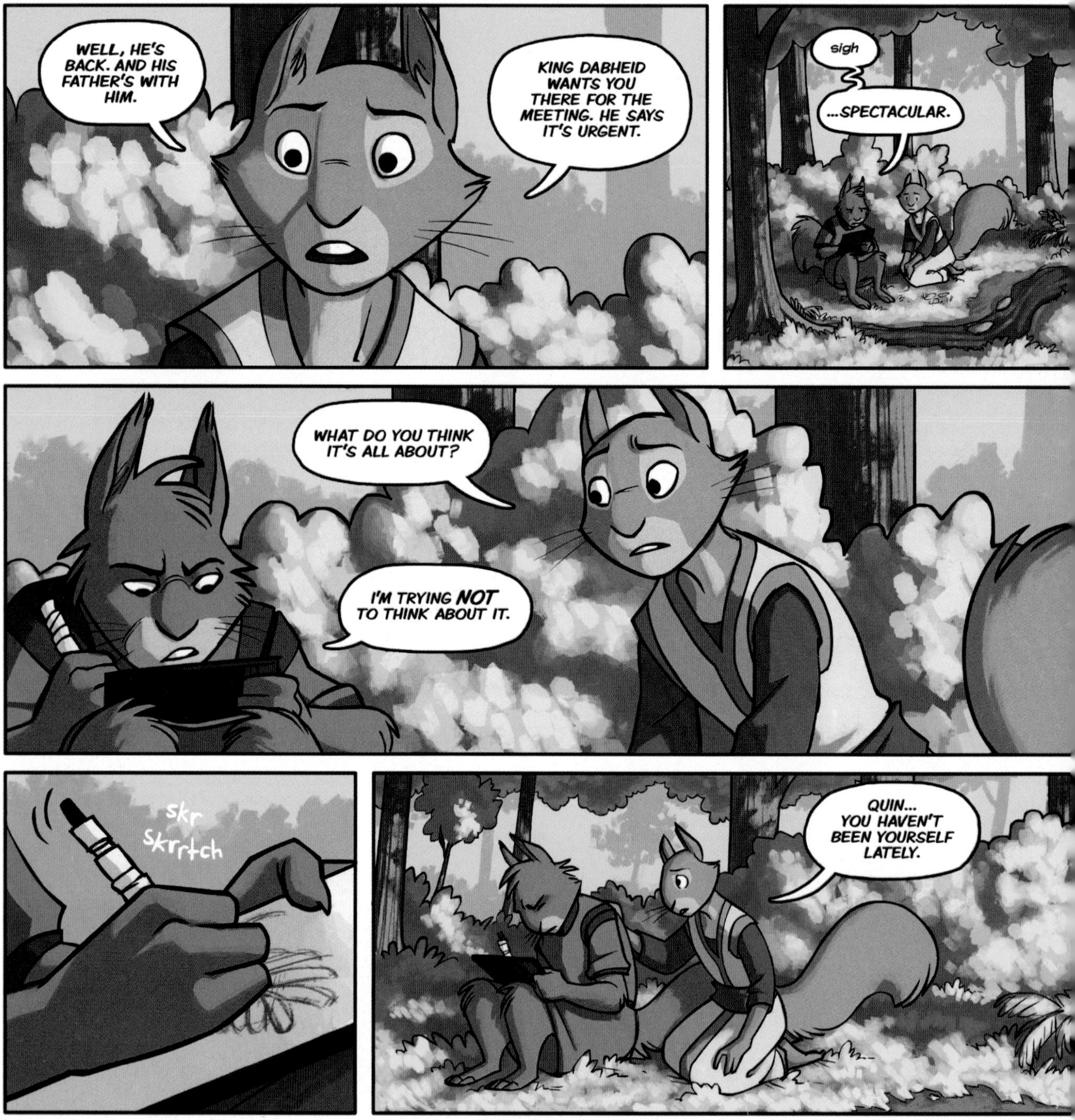
WELL, HE'S BACK. AND HIS FATHER'S WITH HIM.
KING DABHEID WANTS YOU THERE FOR THE MEETING. HE SAYS IT'S URGENT.
sigh
...SPECTACULAR.
WHAT DO YOU THINK IT'S ALL ABOUT?
I'M TRYING **NOT** TO THINK ABOUT IT.
skr
skrrtch
QUIN... YOU HAVEN'T BEEN YOURSELF LATELY.

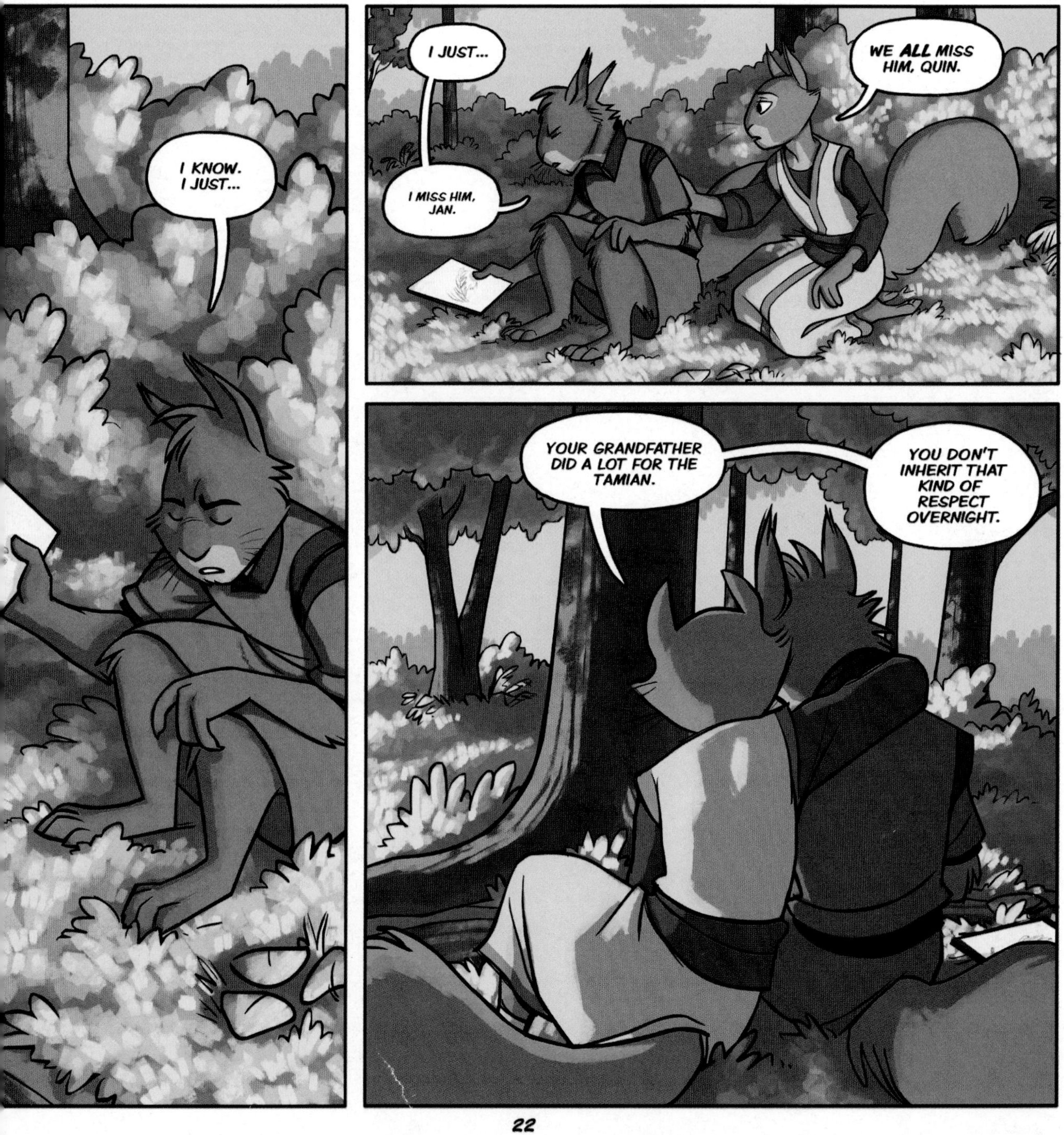

I KNOW.
I JUST...
I JUST...
I MISS HIM, JAN.
WE ALL MISS HIM, QUIN.
YOUR GRANDFATHER DID A LOT FOR THE TAMIAN.
YOU DON'T INHERIT THAT KIND OF RESPECT OVERNIGHT.

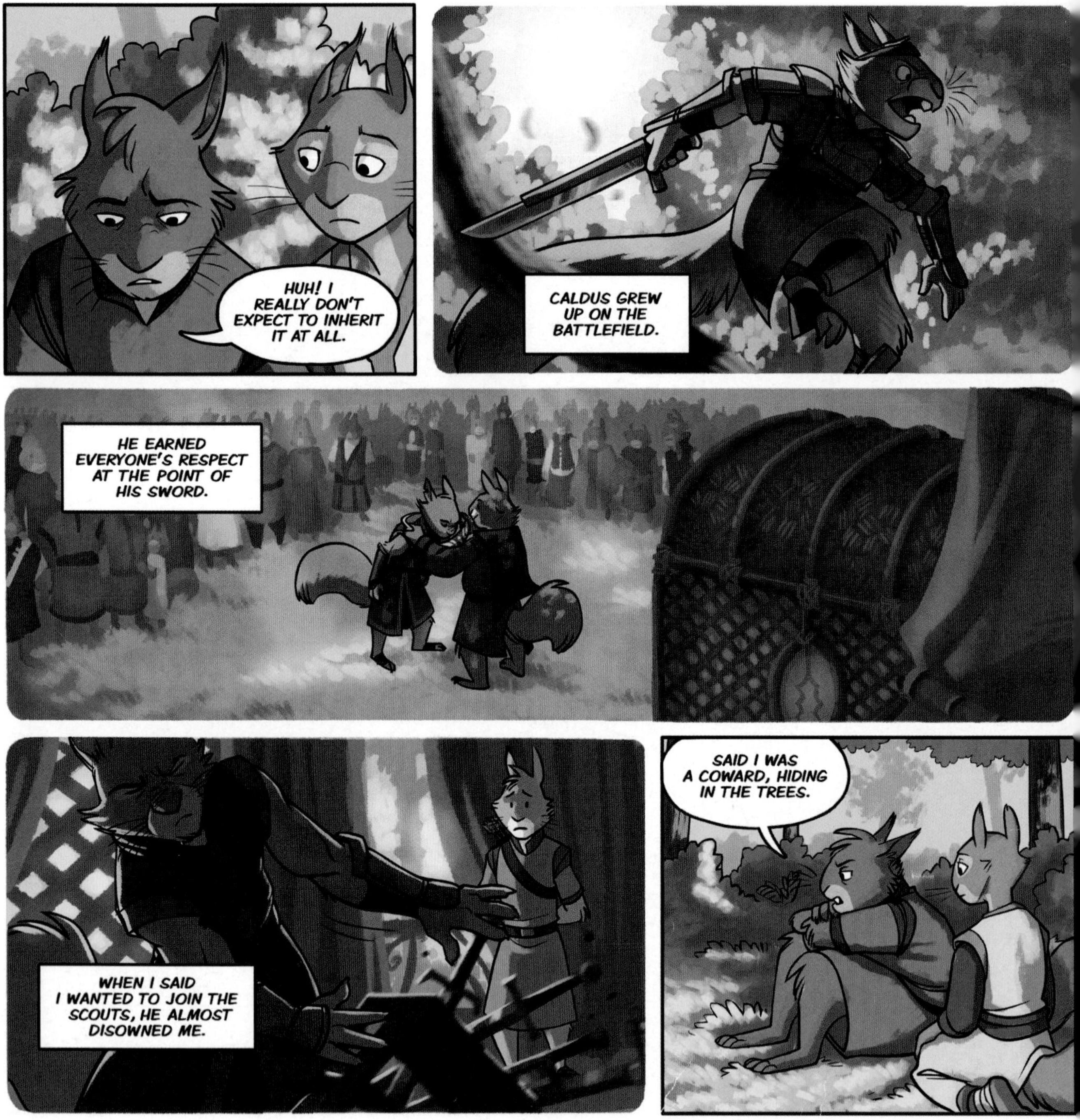
HUH! I REALLY DON'T EXPECT TO INHERIT IT AT ALL.
CALDUS GREW UP ON THE BATTLEFIELD.
HE EARNED EVERYONE'S RESPECT AT THE POINT OF HIS SWORD.
WHEN I SAID I WANTED TO JOIN THE SCOUTS, HE ALMOST DISOWNED ME.
SAID I WAS A COWARD, HIDING IN THE TREES.

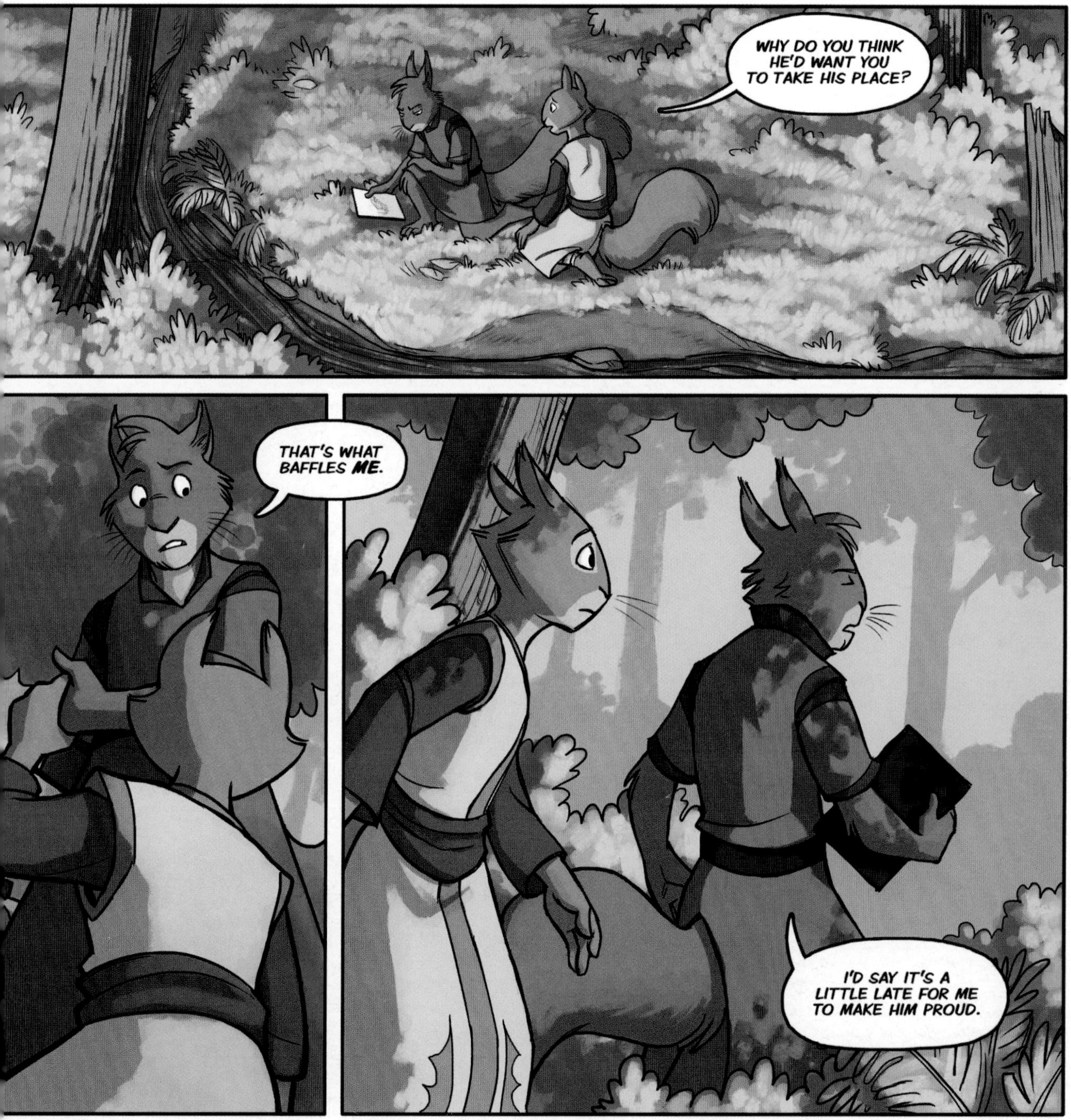
WHY DO YOU THINK HE'D WANT YOU TO TAKE HIS PLACE?
THAT'S WHAT BAFFLES **ME**.
I'D SAY IT'S A LITTLE LATE FOR ME TO MAKE HIM PROUD.

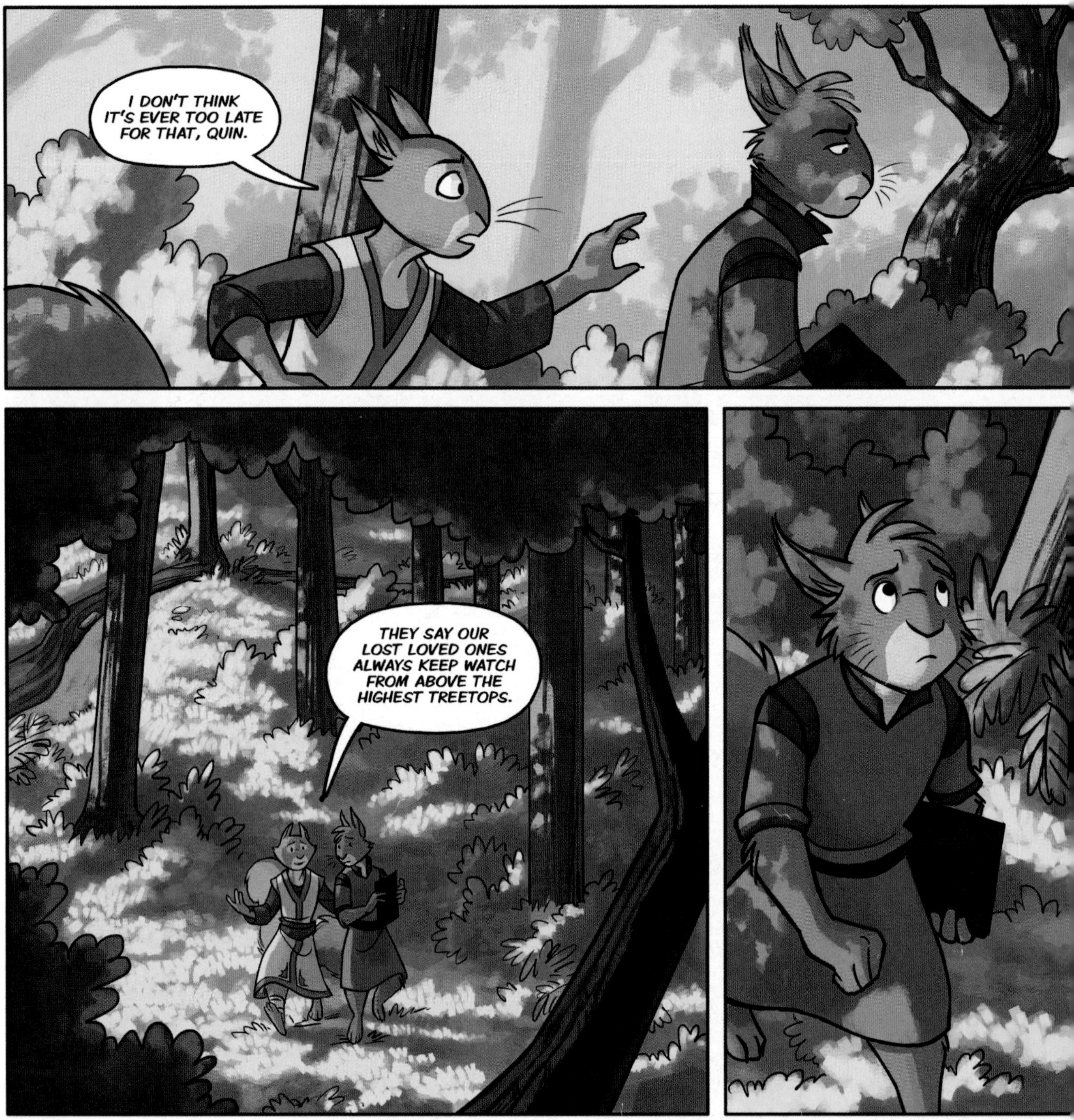
I DON'T THINK IT'S EVER TOO LATE FOR THAT, QUIN.
THEY SAY OUR LOST LOVED ONES ALWAYS KEEP WATCH FROM ABOVE THE HIGHEST TREETOPS.

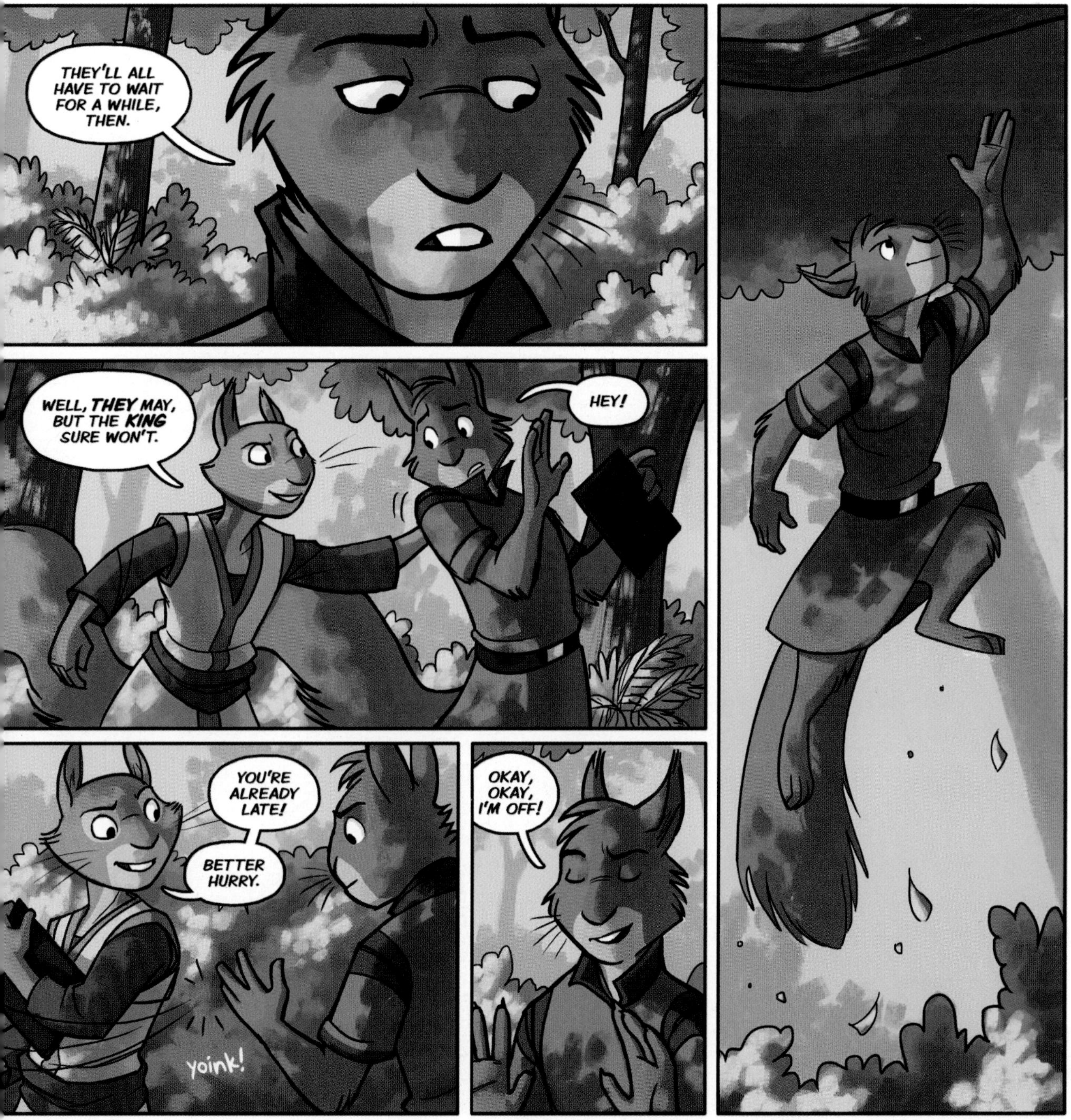
THEY'LL ALL HAVE TO WAIT FOR A WHILE, THEN.
WELL, THEY MAY, BUT THE KING SURE WON'T.
HEY!
YOU'RE ALREADY LATE!
BETTER HURRY.
yoink!
OKAY, OKAY, I'M OFF!

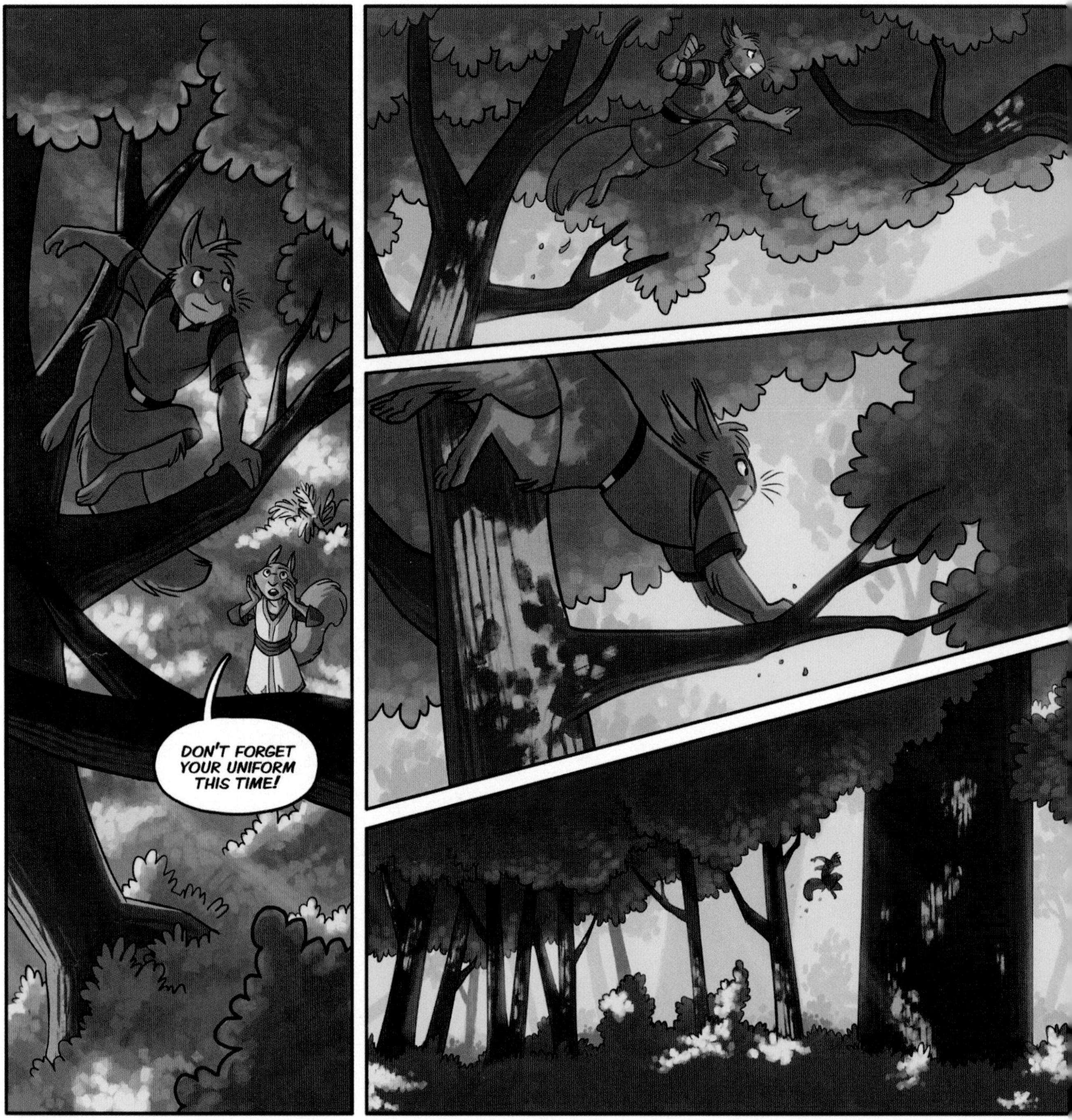
DON'T FORGET YOUR UNIFORM THIS TIME!

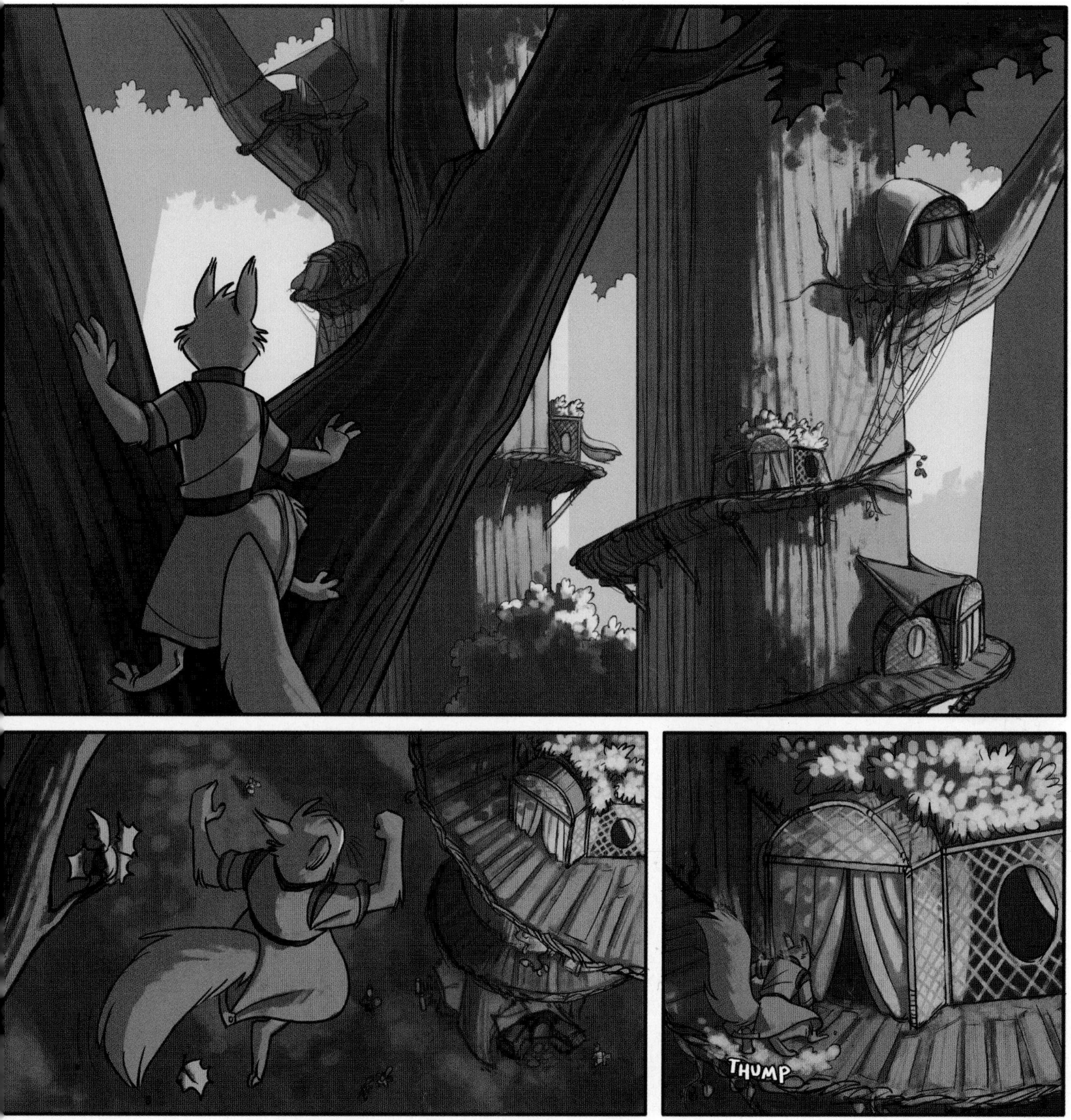
THUMP

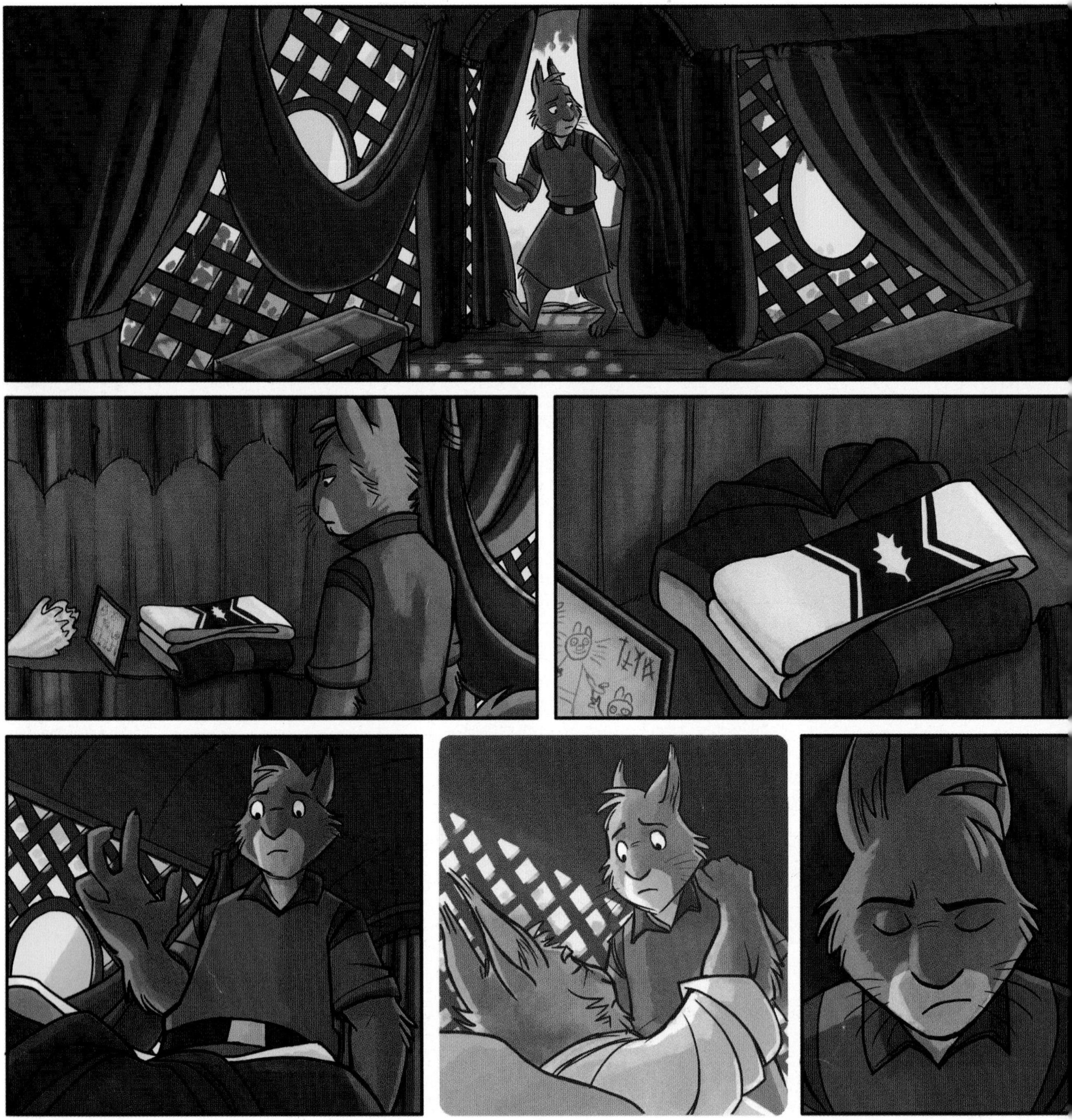

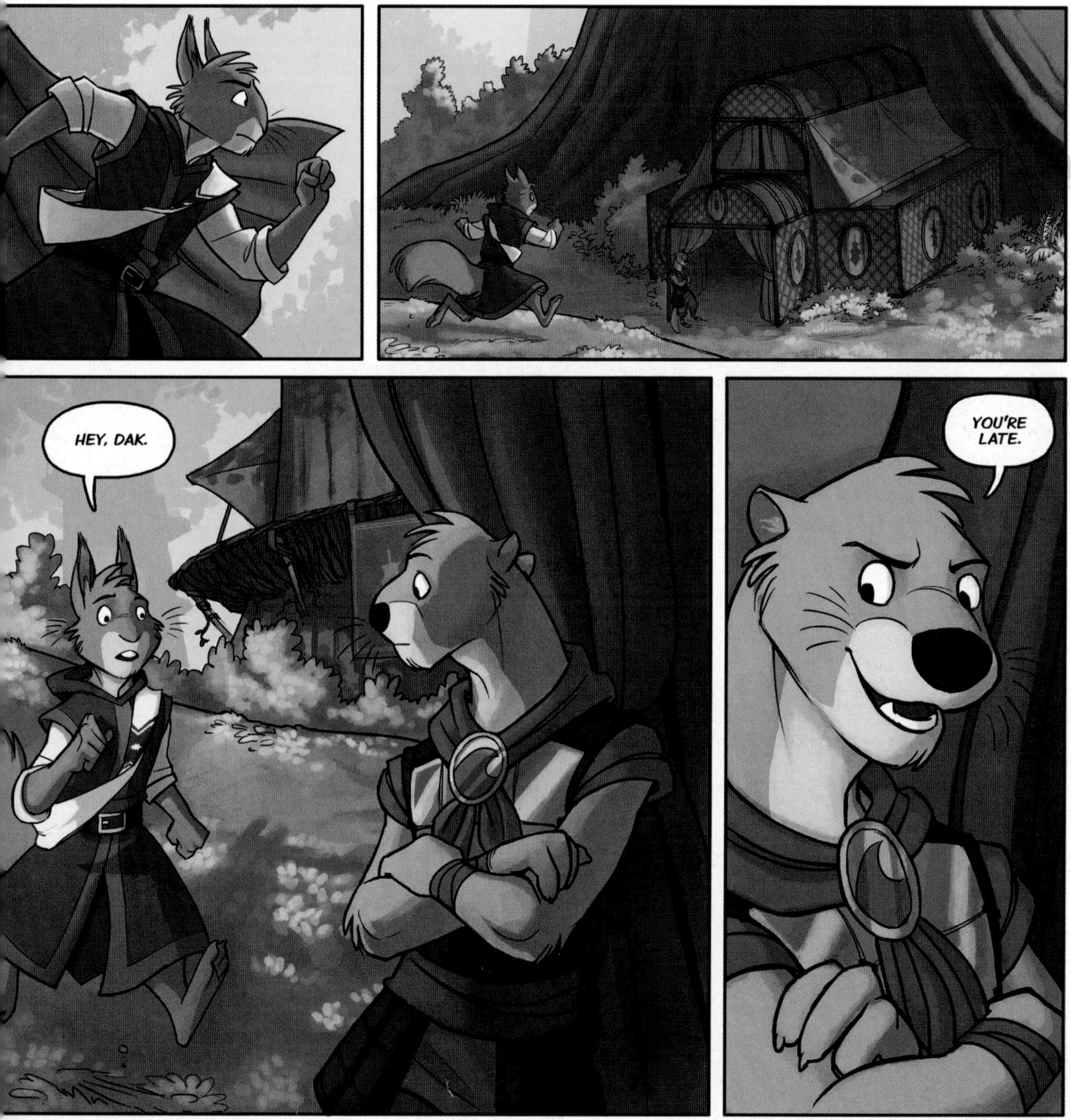
HEY, DAK.
YOU'RE LATE.

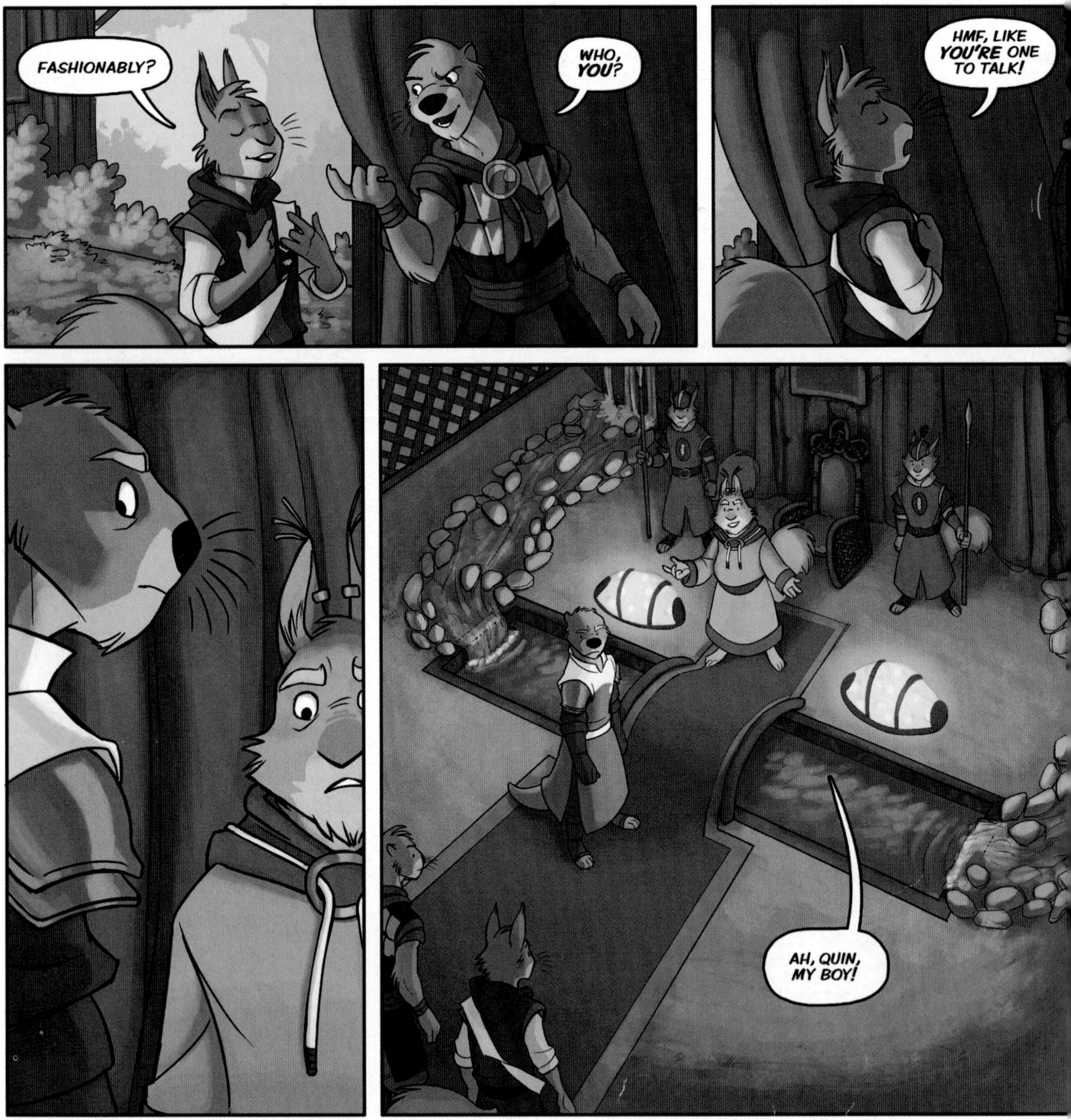
FASHIONABLY?
WHO, YOU?
HMF, LIKE YOU'RE ONE TO TALK!
AH, QUIN, MY BOY!

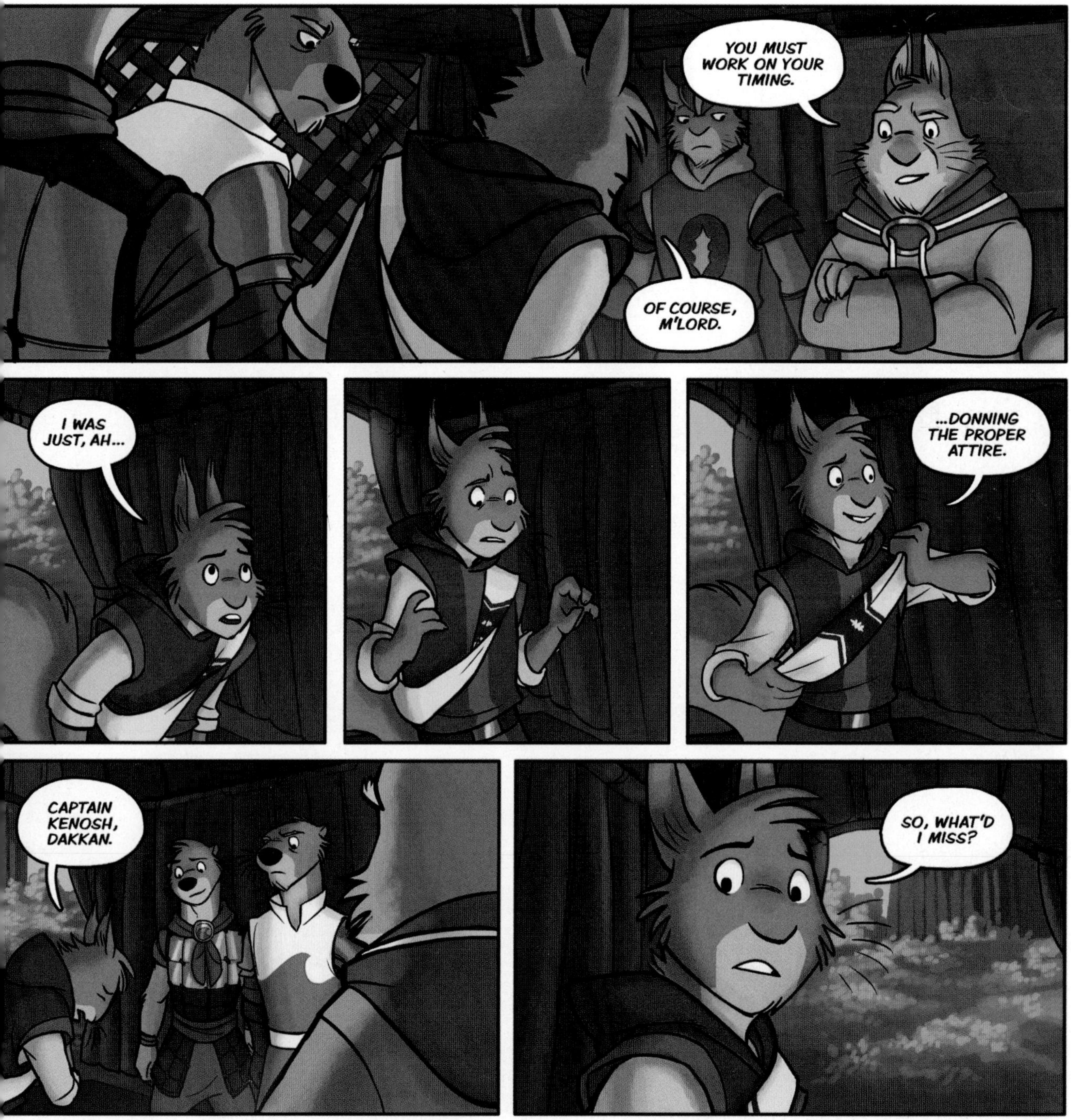
YOU MUST WORK ON YOUR TIMING.
OF COURSE, M'LORD.
I WAS JUST, AH...
...DONNING THE PROPER ATTIRE.
CAPTAIN KENOSH, DAKKAN.
SO, WHAT'D I MISS?

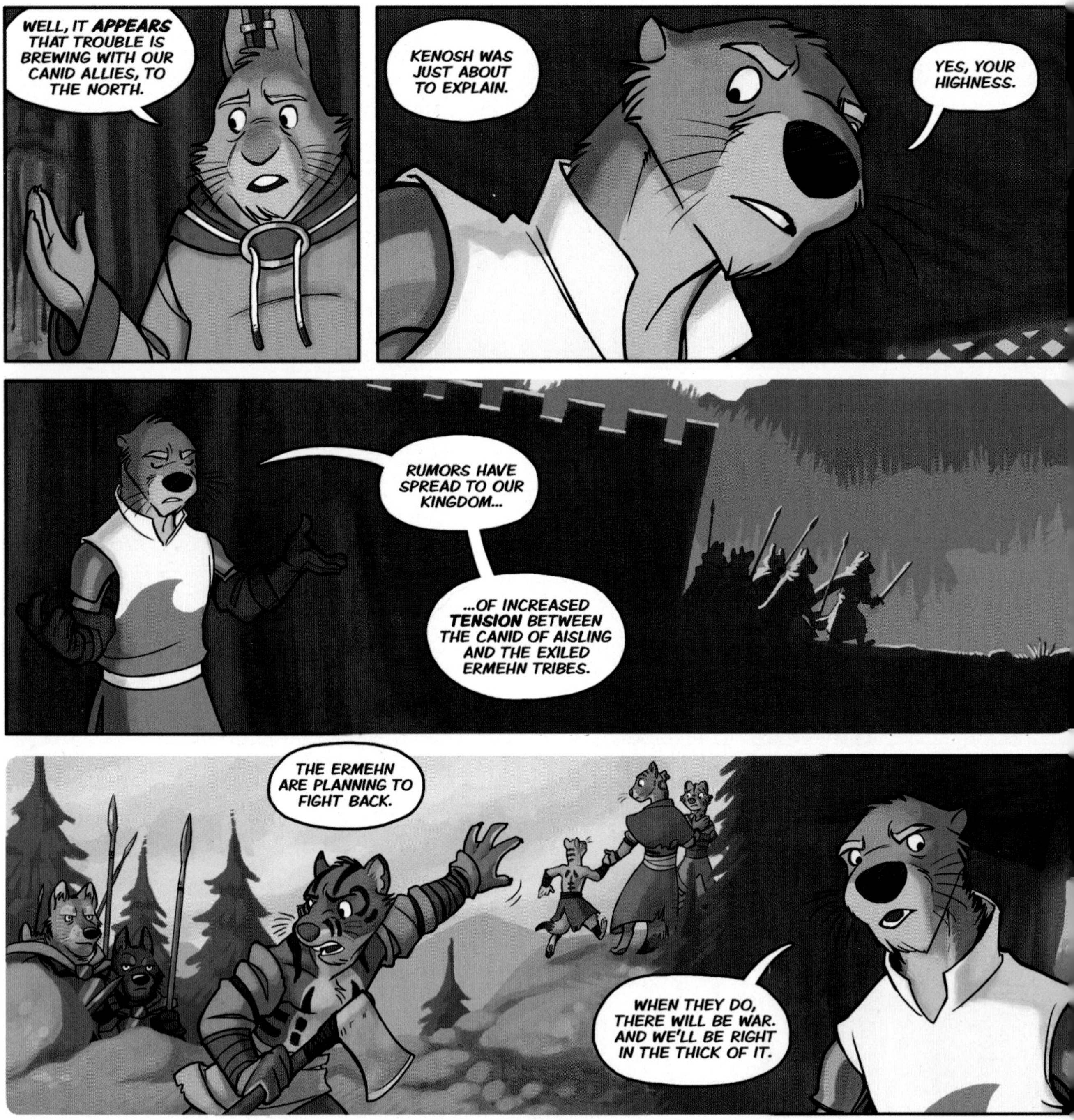
WELL, IT **APPEARS** THAT TROUBLE IS BREWING WITH OUR CANID ALLIES, TO THE NORTH.
KENOSH WAS JUST ABOUT TO EXPLAIN.
YES, YOUR HIGHNESS.
RUMORS HAVE SPREAD TO OUR KINGDOM...
...OF INCREASED **TENSION** BETWEEN THE CANID OF AISLING AND THE EXILED ERMEHN TRIBES.
THE ERMEHN ARE PLANNING TO FIGHT BACK.
WHEN THEY DO, THERE WILL BE WAR. AND WE'LL BE RIGHT IN THE THICK OF IT.

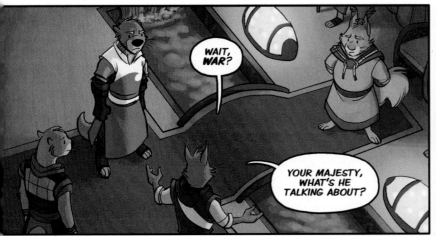

WAIT, *WAR*?

YOUR MAJESTY, WHAT'S HE TALKING ABOUT?

WELL...

WAR, *CAPTAIN*, IS WHAT YOU GET WHEN YOU HAVE TWO ARMIES THAT DON'T LIKE EACH OTHER VERY MUCH.

YES, I KNOW *THAT*.

BUT WHY WOULD *SUNSGROVE* NEED TO GET INVOLVED?

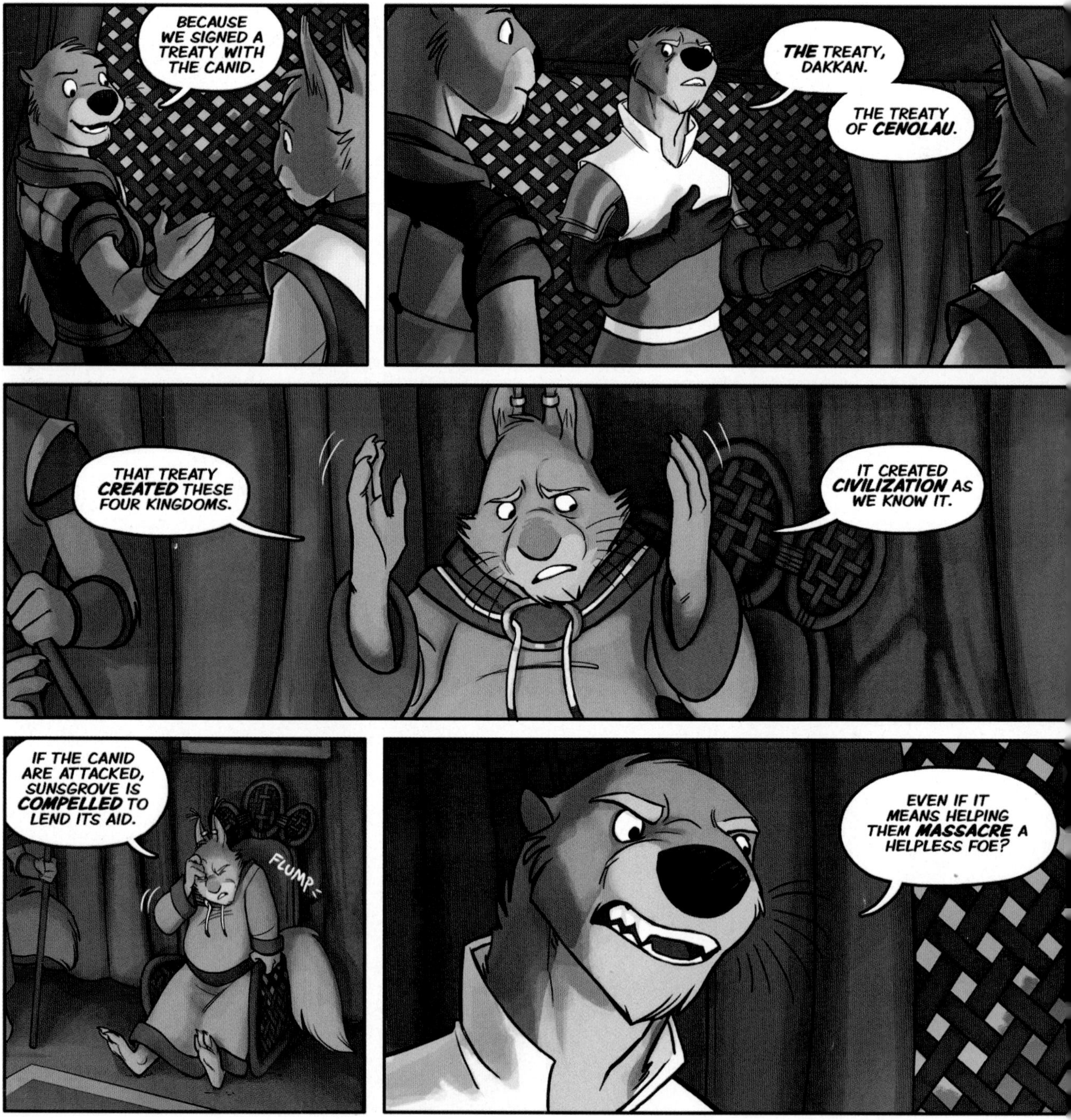
BECAUSE WE SIGNED A TREATY WITH THE CANID.
THE TREATY, DAKKAN.
THE TREATY OF CENOLAU.
THAT TREATY CREATED THESE FOUR KINGDOMS.
IT CREATED CIVILIZATION AS WE KNOW IT.
IF THE CANID ARE ATTACKED, SUNSGROVE IS COMPELLED TO LEND ITS AID.
FLUMP
EVEN IF IT MEANS HELPING THEM MASSACRE A HELPLESS FOE?

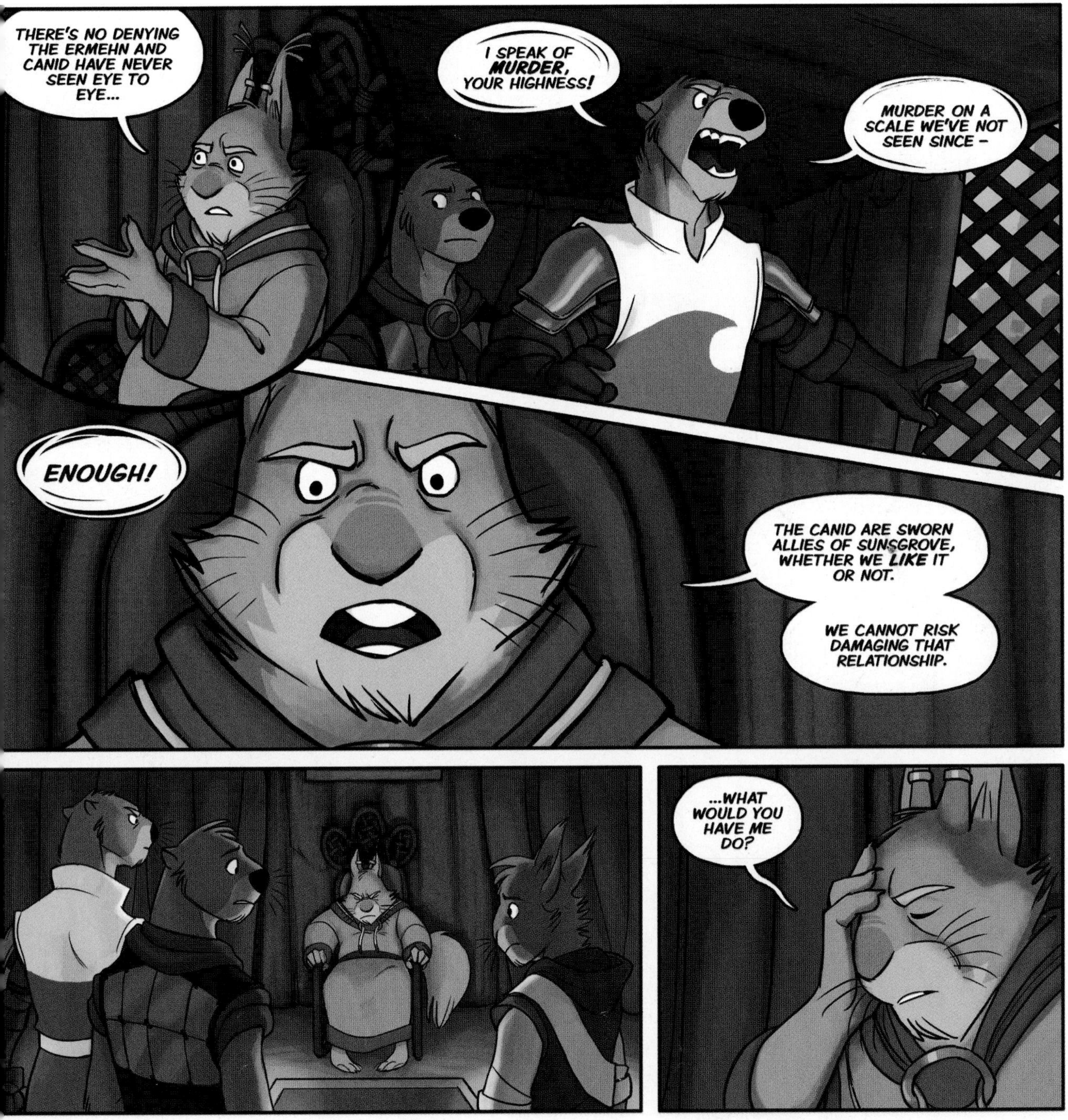
THERE'S NO DENYING THE ERMEHN AND CANID HAVE NEVER SEEN EYE TO EYE...
I SPEAK OF MURDER, YOUR HIGHNESS!
MURDER ON A SCALE WE'VE NOT SEEN SINCE –
ENOUGH!
THE CANID ARE SWORN ALLIES OF SUNSGROVE, WHETHER WE LIKE IT OR NOT.
WE CANNOT RISK DAMAGING THAT RELATIONSHIP.
...WHAT WOULD YOU HAVE ME DO?

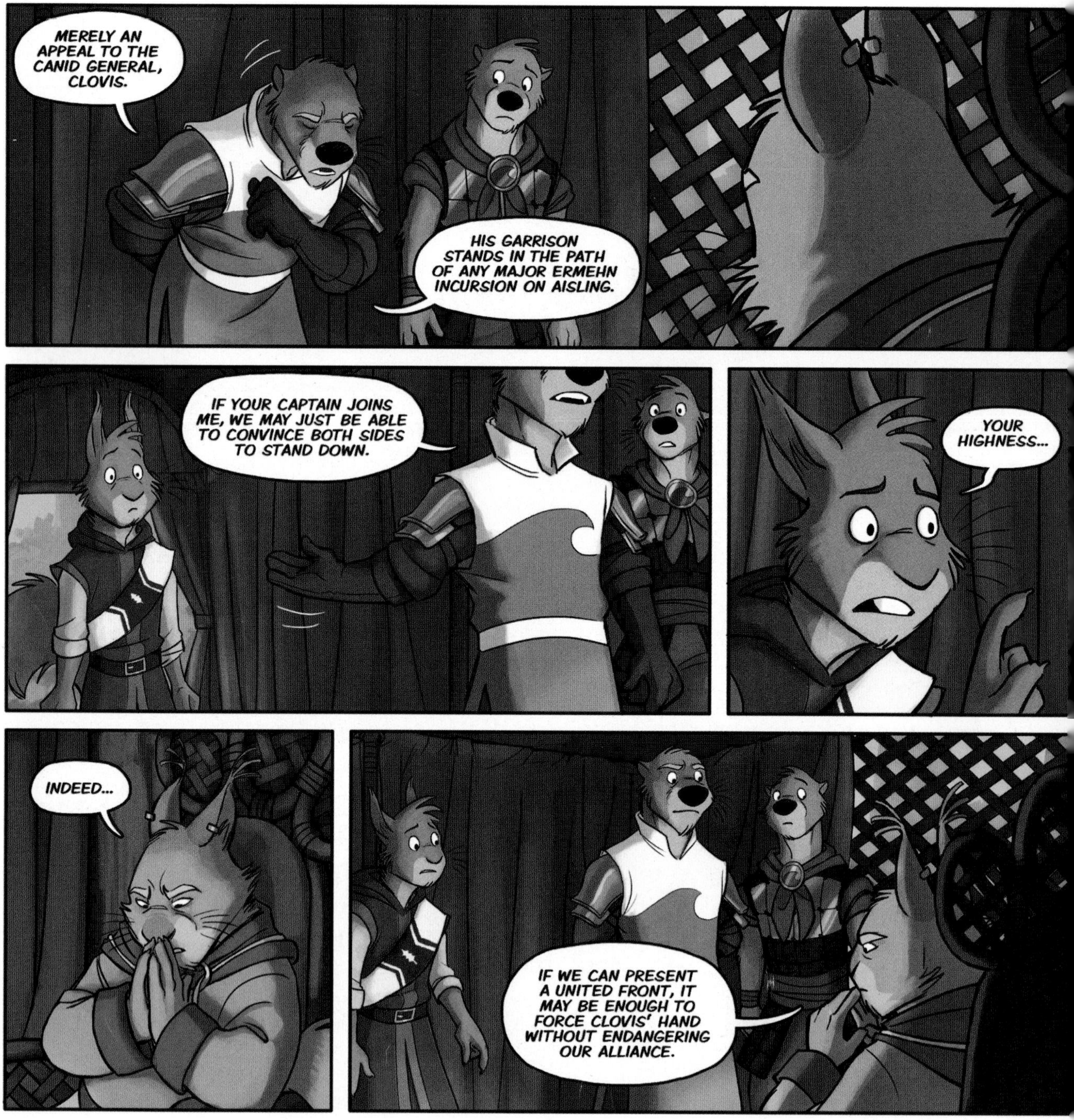
MERELY AN APPEAL TO THE CANID GENERAL, CLOVIS.
HIS GARRISON STANDS IN THE PATH OF ANY MAJOR ERMEHN INCURSION ON AISLING.
IF YOUR CAPTAIN JOINS ME, WE MAY JUST BE ABLE TO CONVINCE BOTH SIDES TO STAND DOWN.
YOUR HIGHNESS...
INDEED...
IF WE CAN PRESENT A UNITED FRONT, IT MAY BE ENOUGH TO FORCE CLOVIS' HAND WITHOUT ENDANGERING OUR ALLIANCE.

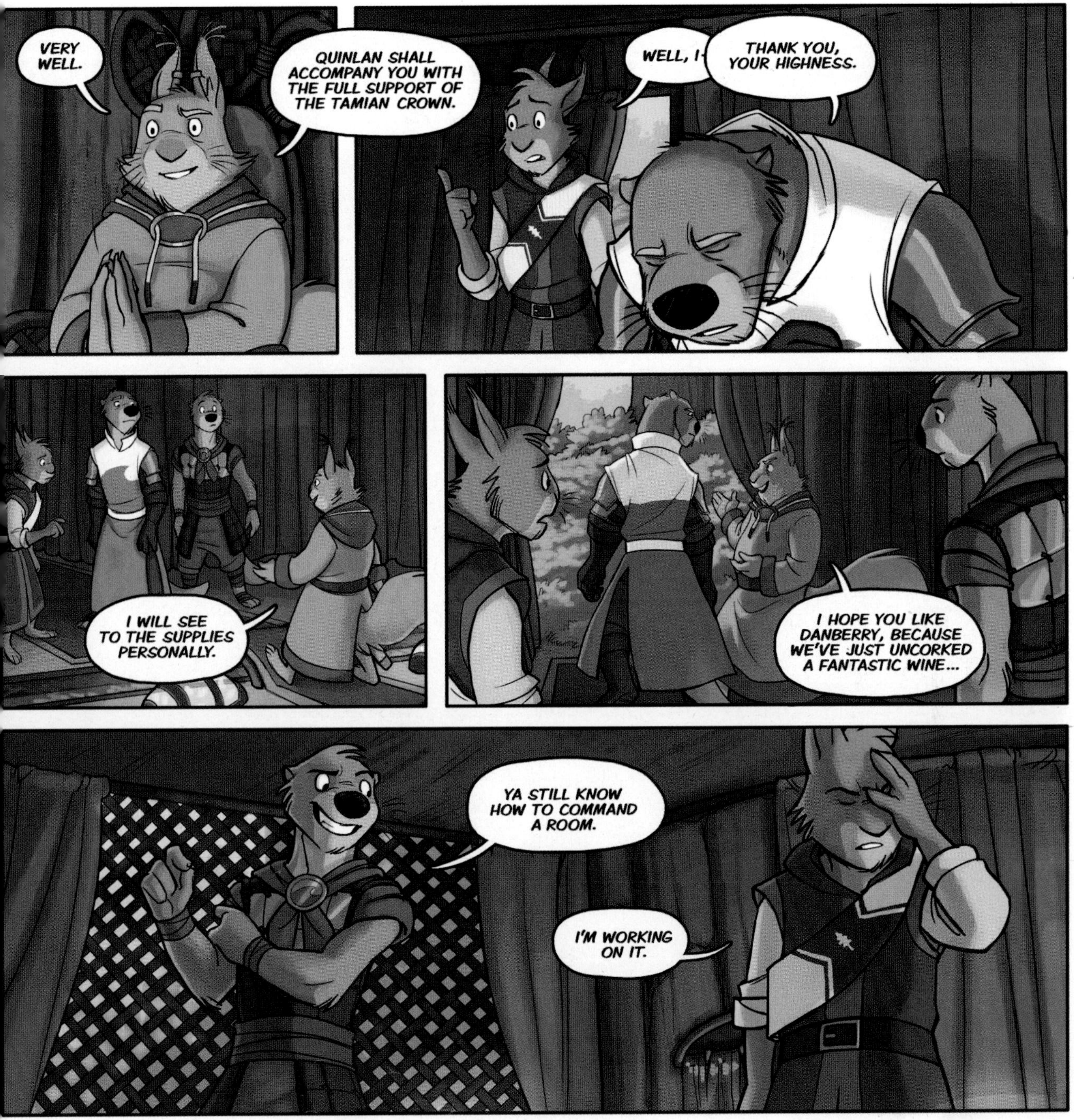
VERY WELL.
QUINLAN SHALL ACCOMPANY YOU WITH THE FULL SUPPORT OF THE TAMIAN CROWN.
WELL, I-
THANK YOU, YOUR HIGHNESS.
I WILL SEE TO THE SUPPLIES PERSONALLY.
I HOPE YOU LIKE DANBERRY, BECAUSE WE'VE JUST UNCORKED A FANTASTIC WINE...
YA STILL KNOW HOW TO COMMAND A ROOM.
I'M WORKING ON IT.

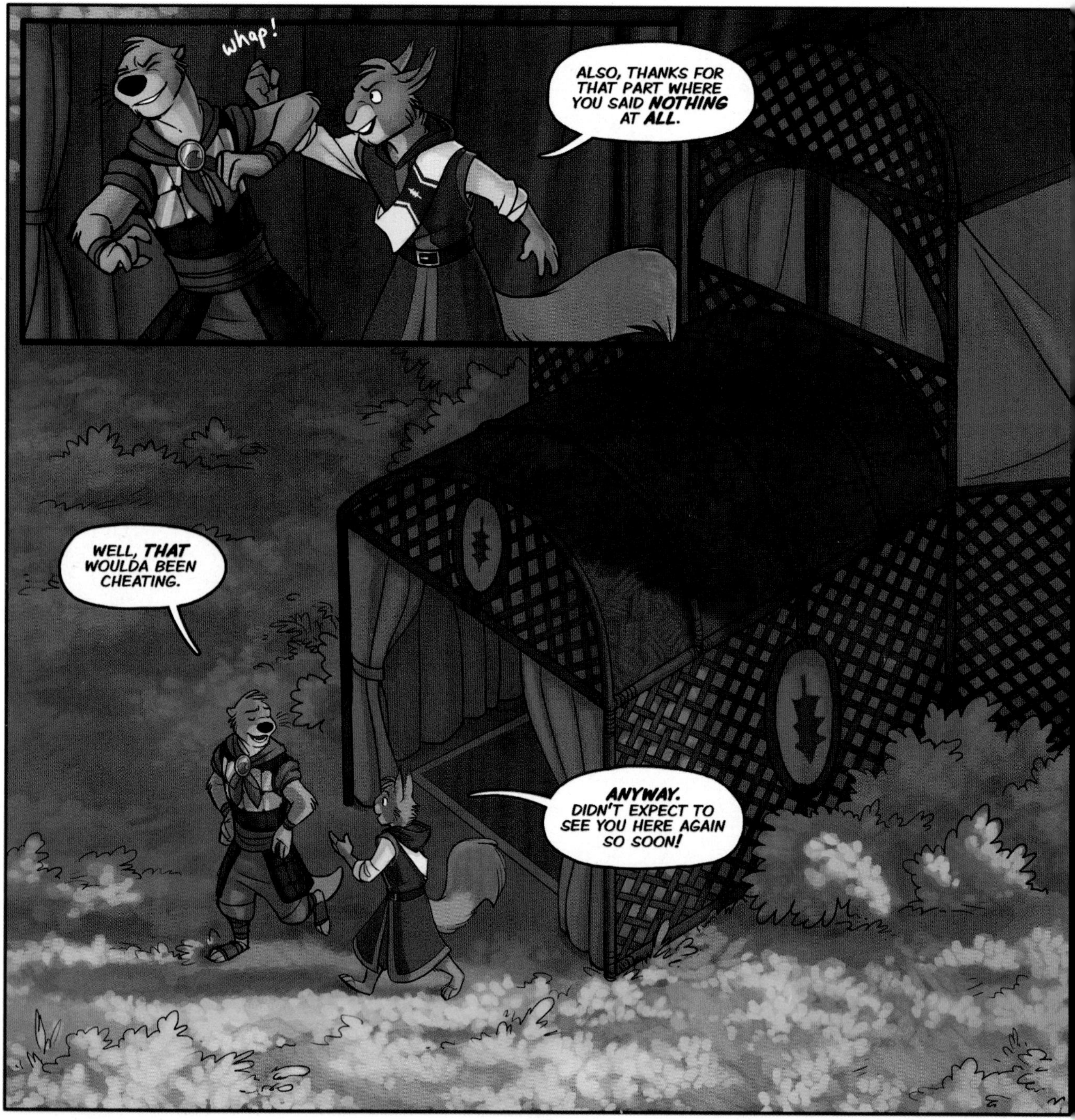
whap!
ALSO, THANKS FOR THAT PART WHERE YOU SAID NOTHING AT ALL.
WELL, THAT WOULDA BEEN CHEATING.
ANYWAY. DIDN'T EXPECT TO SEE YOU HERE AGAIN SO SOON!

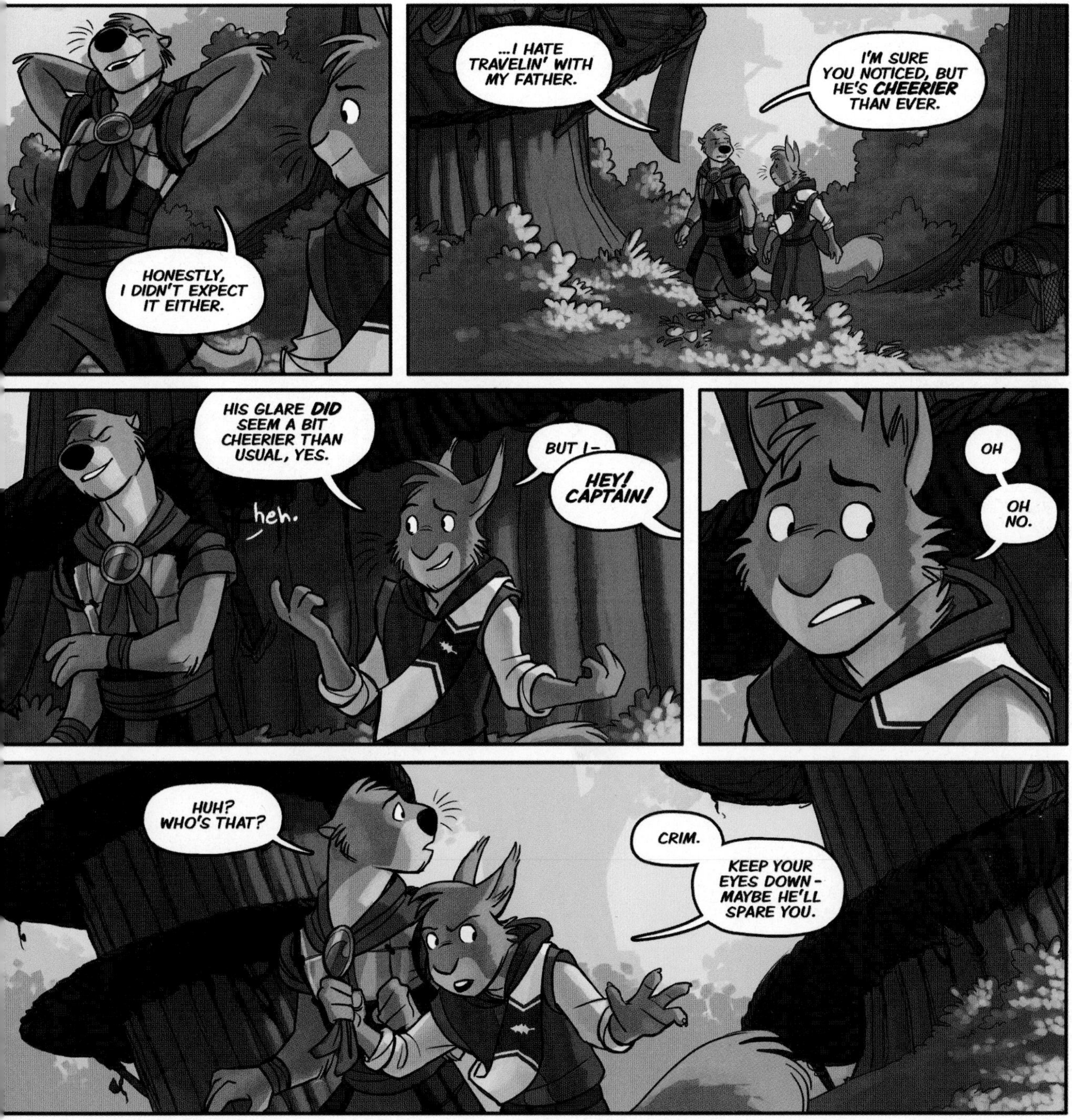
HONESTLY, I DIDN'T EXPECT IT EITHER.
...I HATE TRAVELIN' WITH MY FATHER.
I'M SURE YOU NOTICED, BUT HE'S **CHEERIER** THAN EVER.
HIS GLARE **DID** SEEM A BIT CHEERIER THAN USUAL, YES.
heh.
BUT I—
HEY! CAPTAIN!
OH
OH NO.
HUH? WHO'S THAT?
CRIM.
KEEP YOUR EYES DOWN - MAYBE HE'LL SPARE YOU.

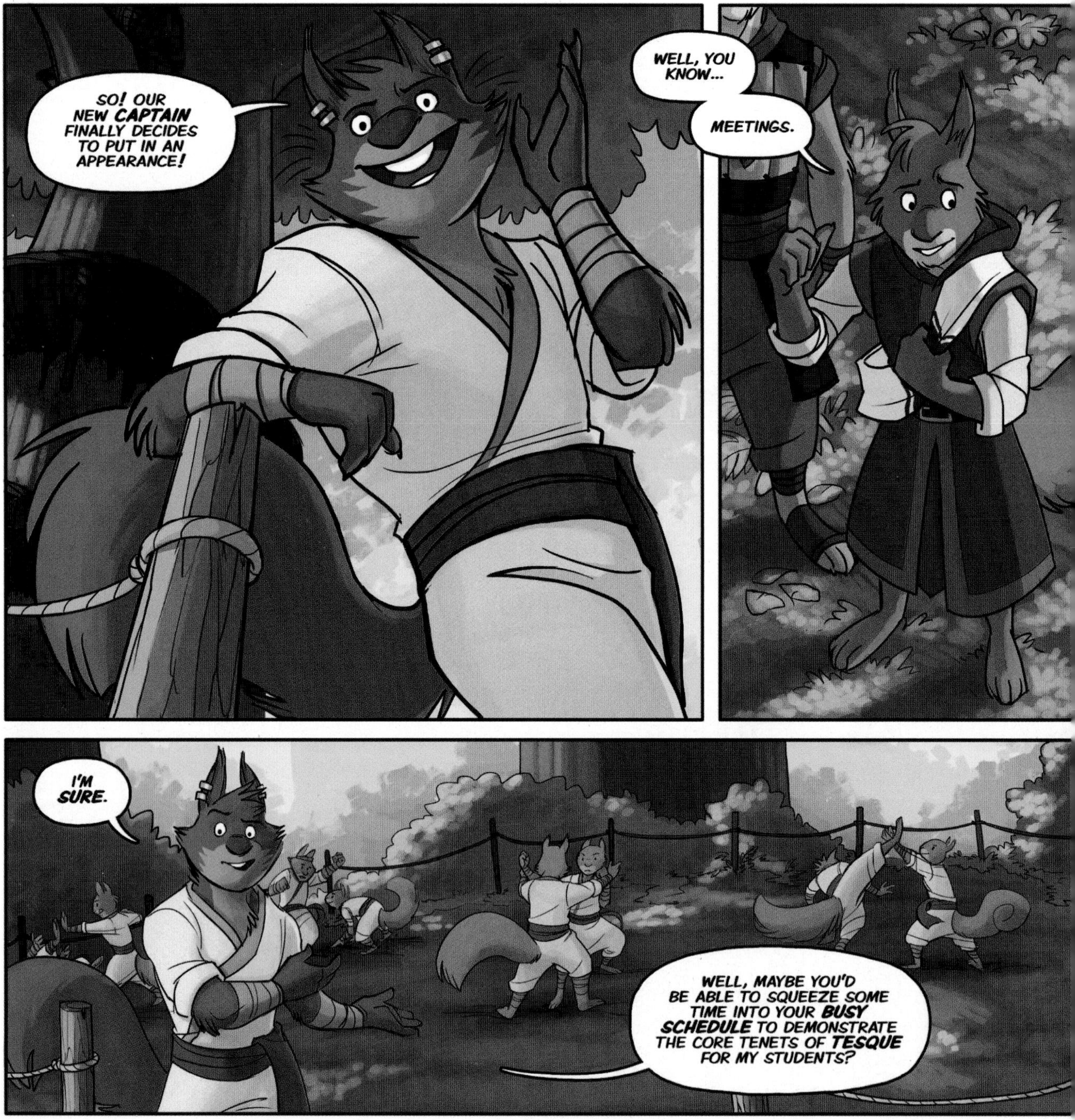

SO! OUR NEW CAPTAIN FINALLY DECIDES TO PUT IN AN APPEARANCE!
WELL, YOU KNOW...
MEETINGS.
I'M SURE.
WELL, MAYBE YOU'D BE ABLE TO SQUEEZE SOME TIME INTO YOUR BUSY SCHEDULE TO DEMONSTRATE THE CORE TENETS OF TESQUE FOR MY STUDENTS?

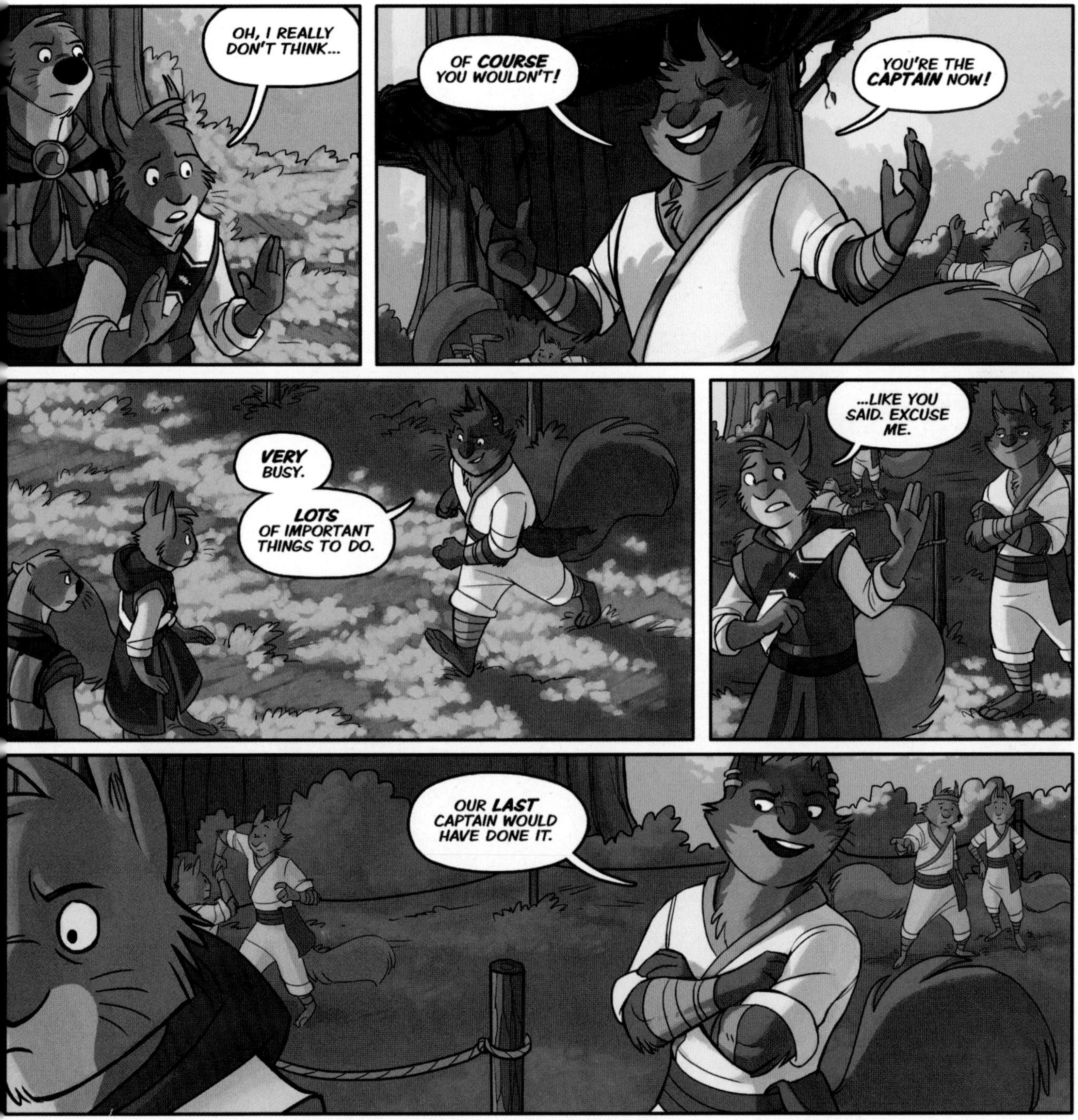
OH, I REALLY DON'T THINK...
OF COURSE YOU WOULDN'T!
YOU'RE THE CAPTAIN NOW!
VERY BUSY.
LOTS OF IMPORTANT THINGS TO DO.
...LIKE YOU SAID. EXCUSE ME.
OUR LAST CAPTAIN WOULD HAVE DONE IT.

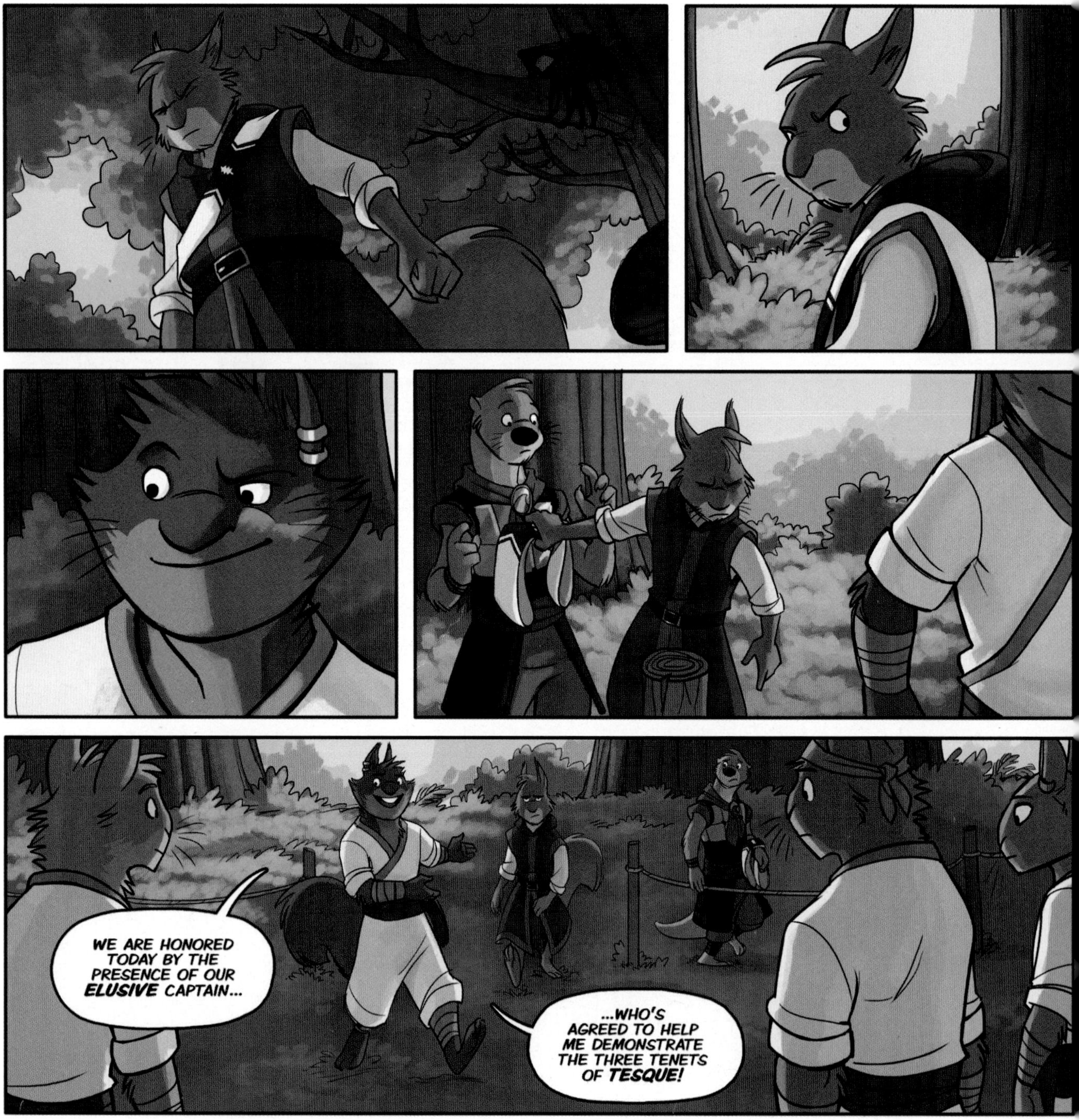
WE ARE HONORED TODAY BY THE PRESENCE OF OUR ELUSIVE CAPTAIN...
...WHO'S AGREED TO HELP ME DEMONSTRATE THE THREE TENETS OF TESQUE!

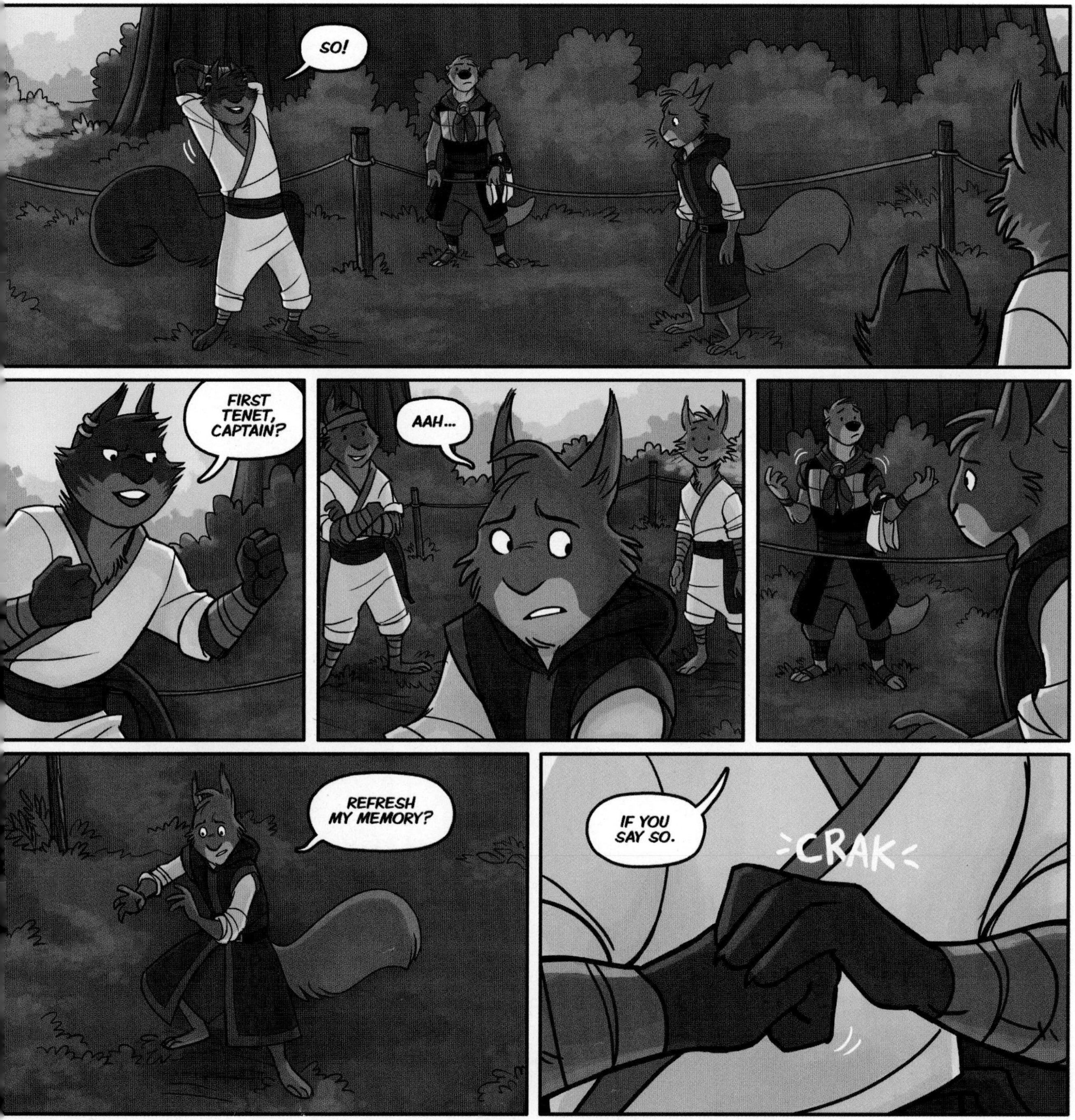
SO!
FIRST TENET, CAPTAIN?
AAH...
REFRESH MY MEMORY?
IF YOU SAY SO.
CRAK

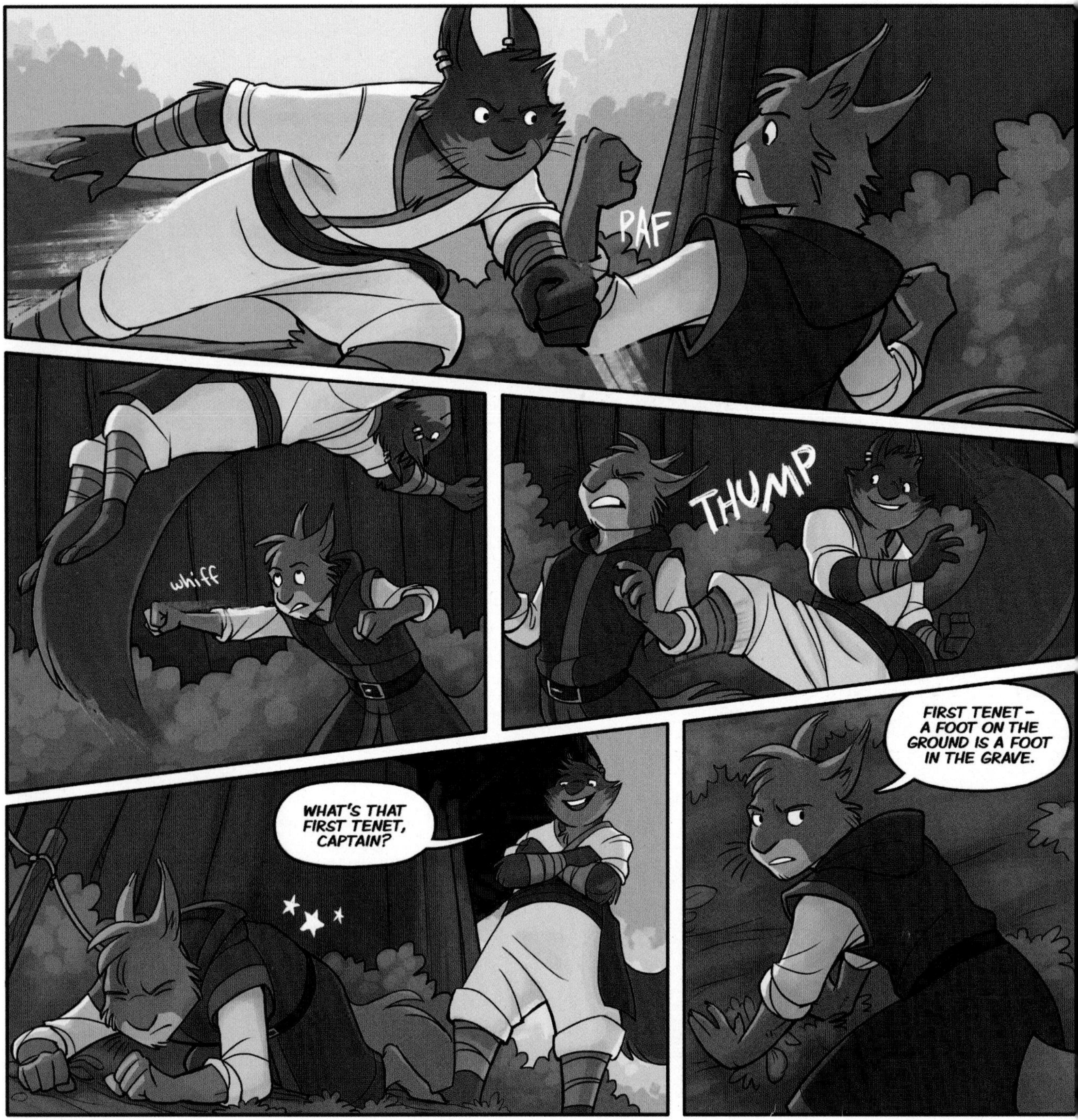
PAF
whiff
THUMP
FIRST TENET – A FOOT ON THE GROUND IS A FOOT IN THE GRAVE.
WHAT'S THAT FIRST TENET, CAPTAIN?

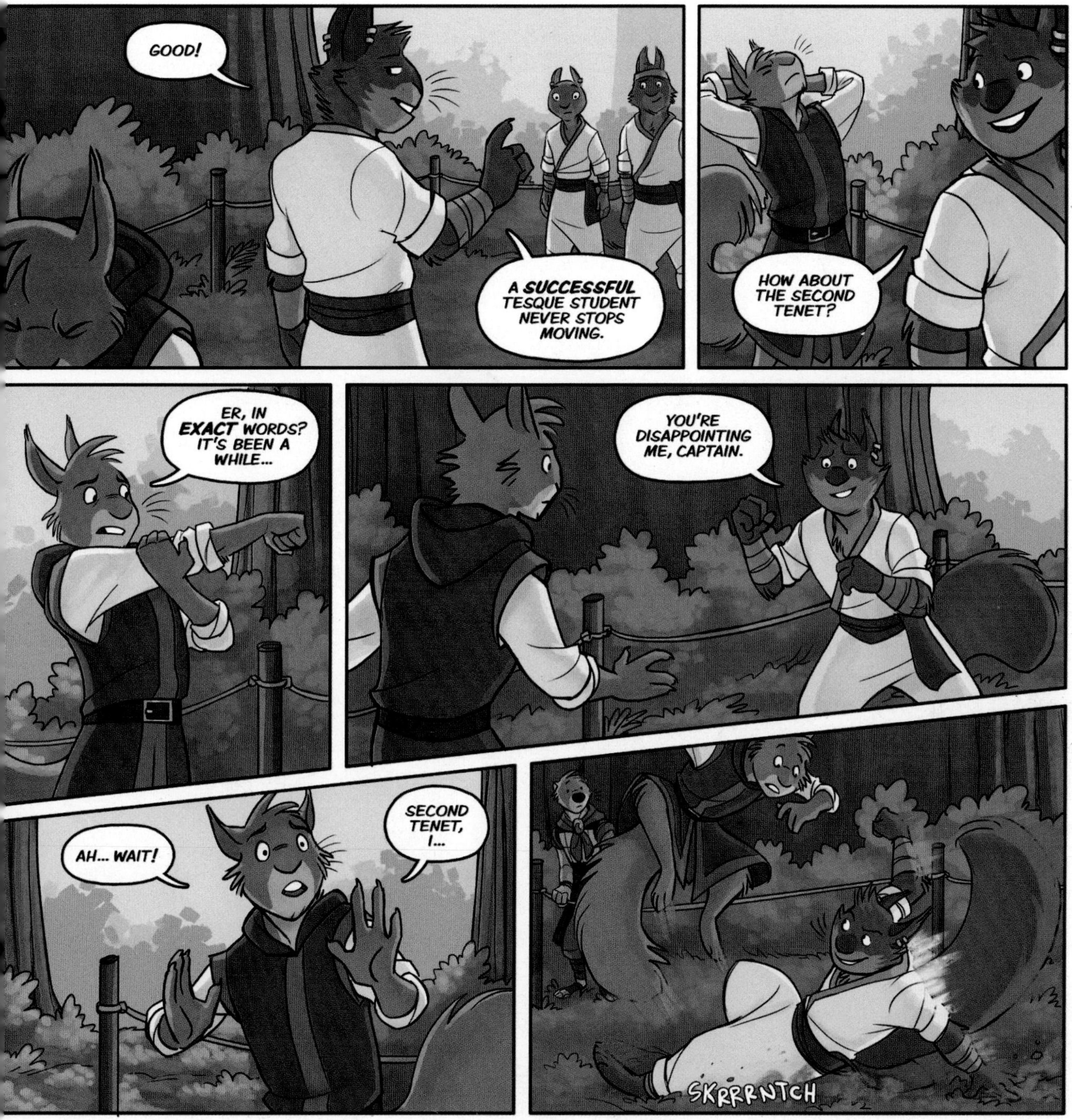
GOOD!
A SUCCESSFUL TESQUE STUDENT NEVER STOPS MOVING.
HOW ABOUT THE SECOND TENET?
ER, IN EXACT WORDS? IT'S BEEN A WHILE...
YOU'RE DISAPPOINTING ME, CAPTAIN.
AH... WAIT!
SECOND TENET, I...
SKRRRNTCH

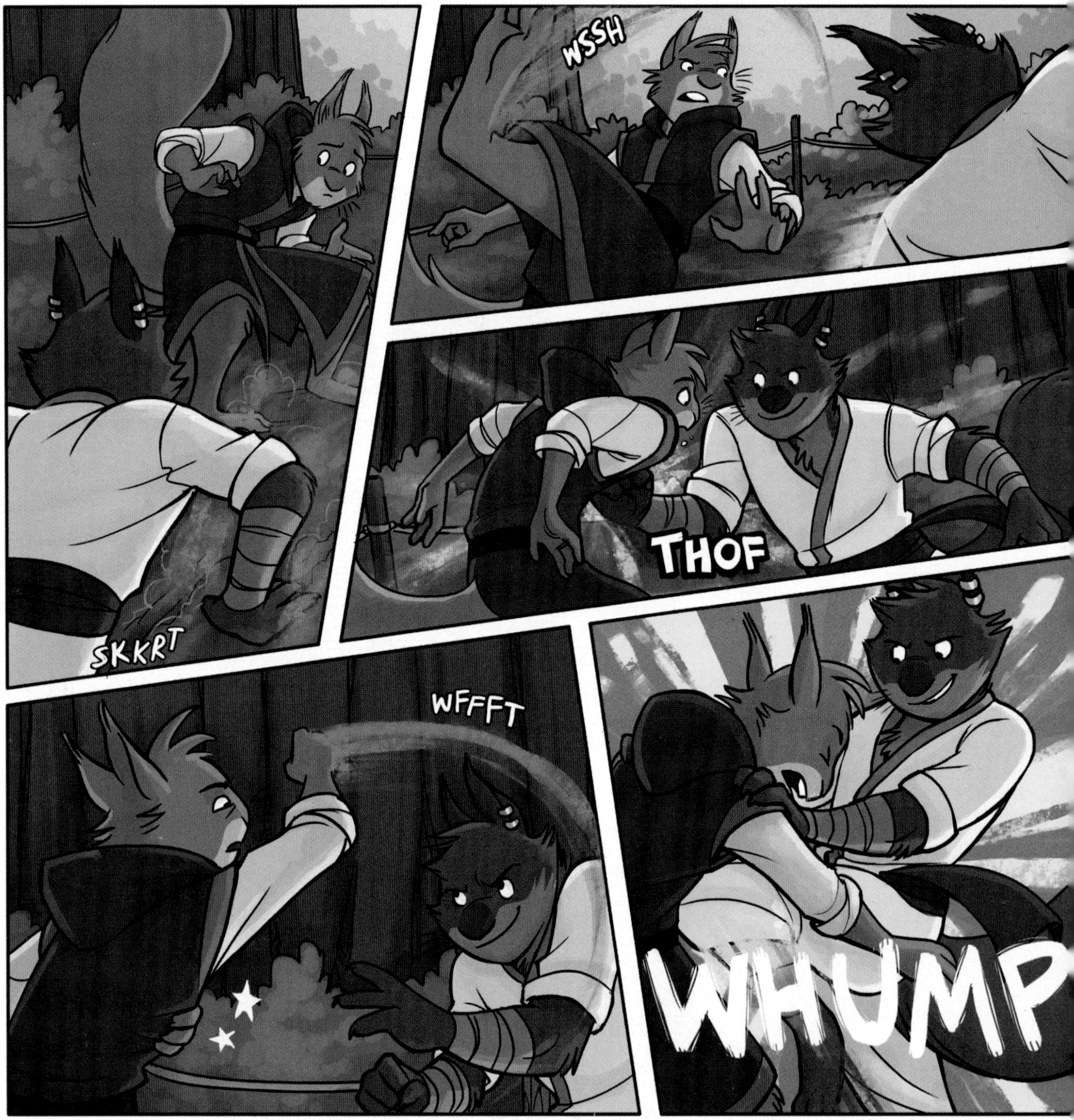
SKKRT
WSSH
THOF
WFFFT
WHUMP

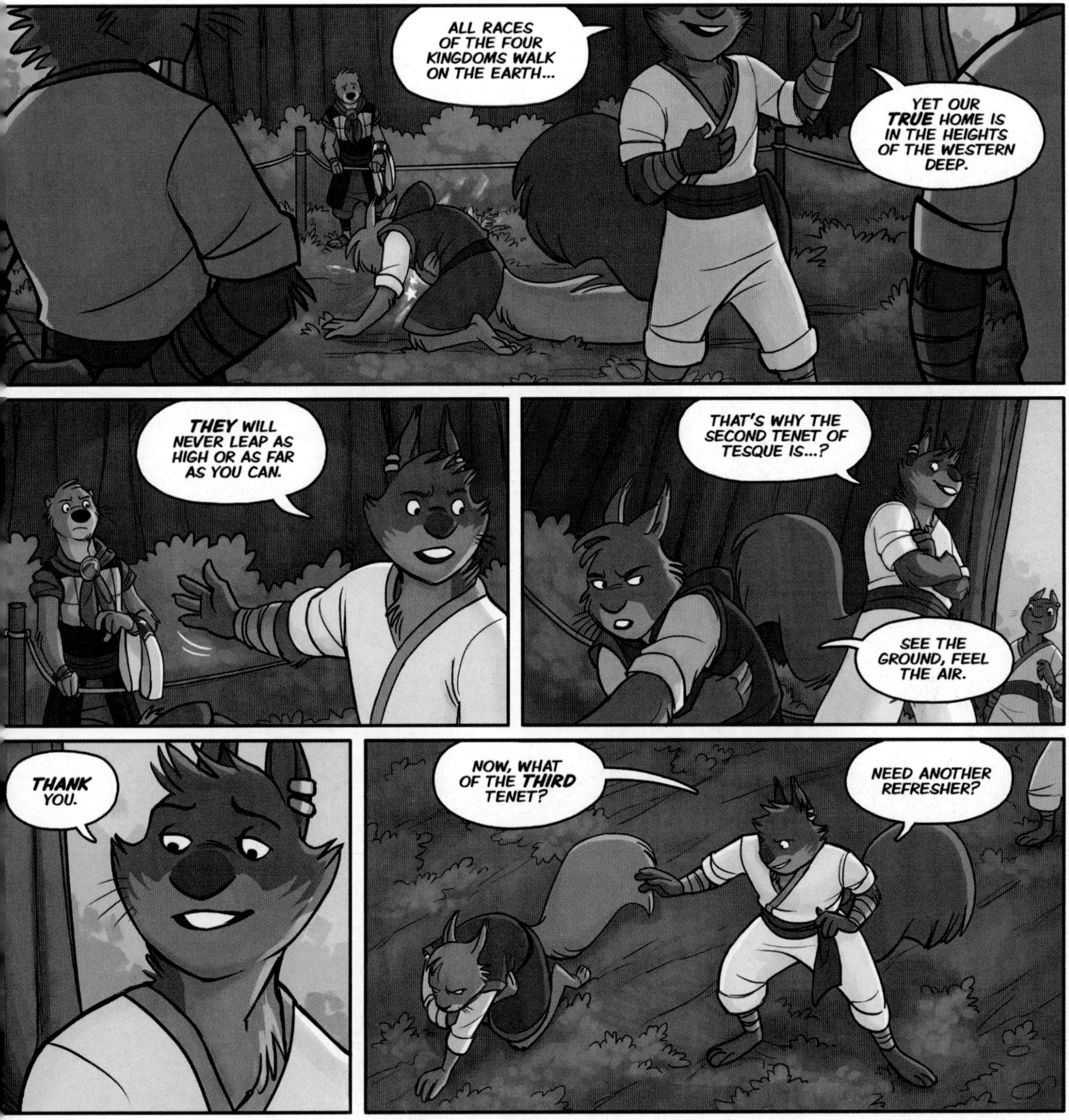
ALL RACES OF THE FOUR KINGDOMS WALK ON THE EARTH...
YET OUR TRUE HOME IS IN THE HEIGHTS OF THE WESTERN DEEP.
THEY WILL NEVER LEAP AS HIGH OR AS FAR AS YOU CAN.
THAT'S WHY THE SECOND TENET OF TESQUE IS...?
SEE THE GROUND, FEEL THE AIR.
THANK YOU.
NOW, WHAT OF THE THIRD TENET?
NEED ANOTHER REFRESHER?

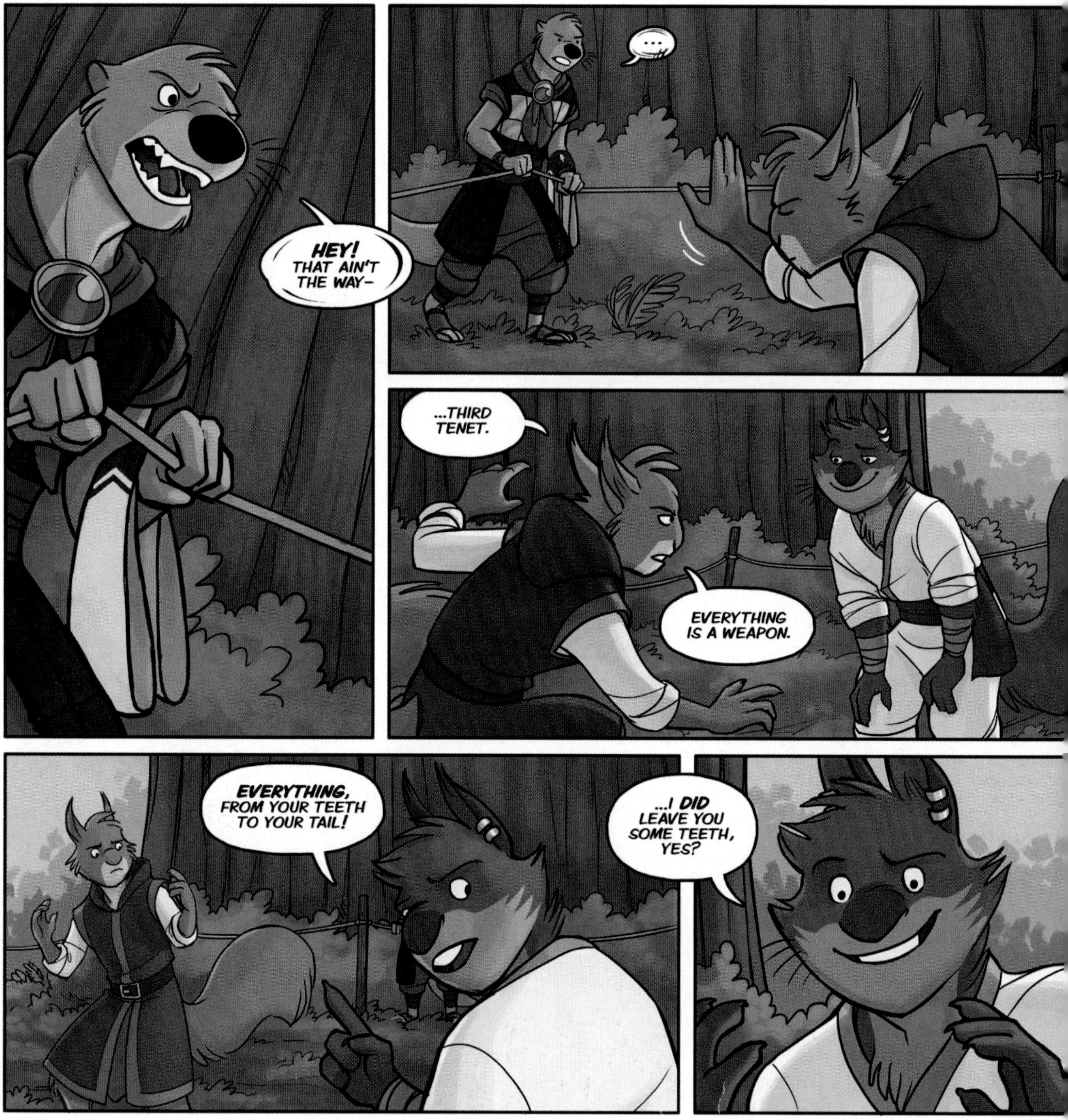
HEY! THAT AIN'T THE WAY-
...
...THIRD TENET.
EVERYTHING IS A WEAPON.
EVERYTHING, FROM YOUR TEETH TO YOUR TAIL!
...I DID LEAVE YOU SOME TEETH, YES?

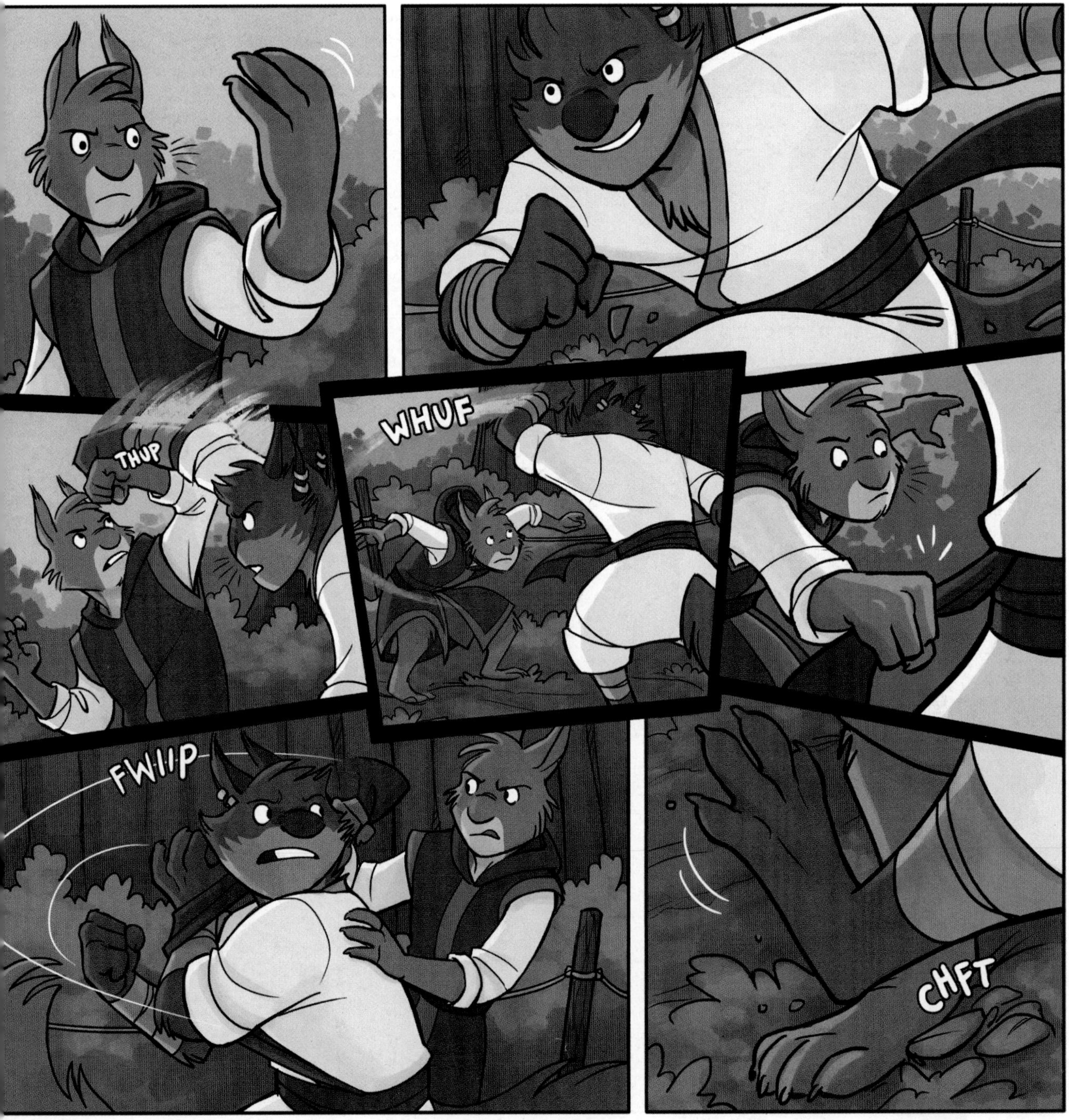
THUP
WHUF
FWIIP
CHFT

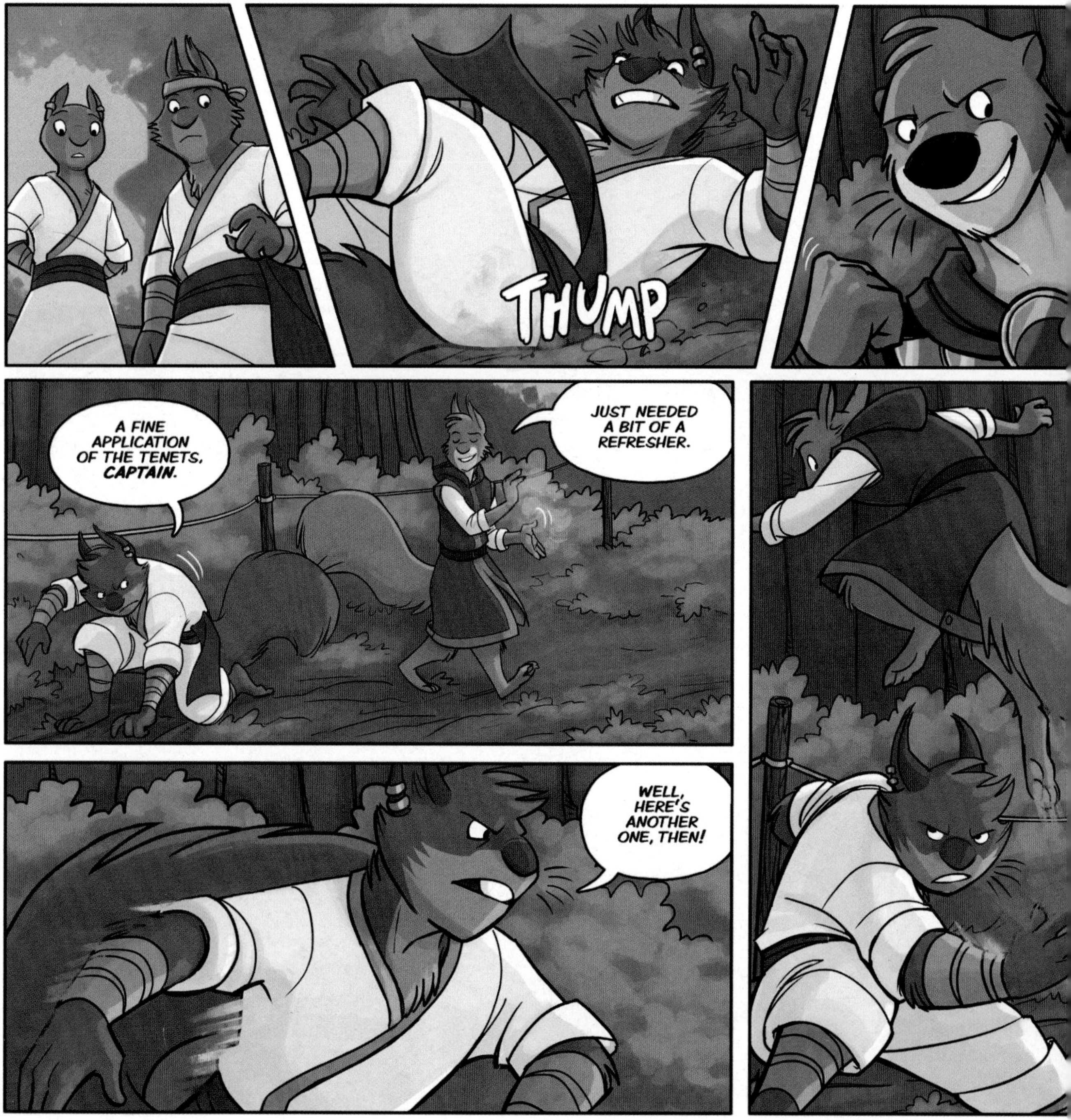
THUMP
A FINE APPLICATION OF THE TENETS, CAPTAIN.
JUST NEEDED A BIT OF A REFRESHER.
WELL, HERE'S ANOTHER ONE, THEN!

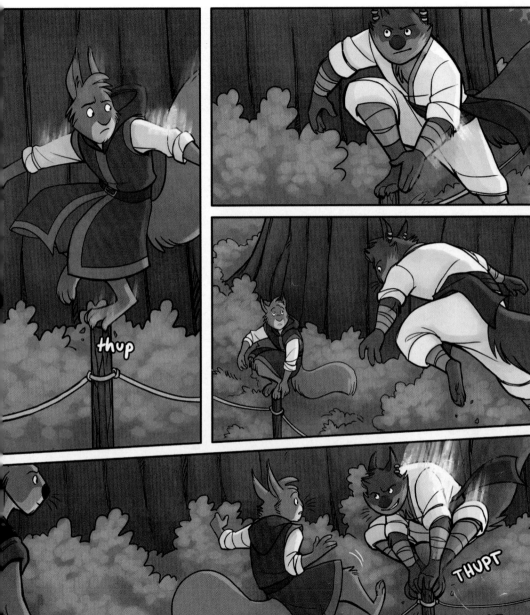

thup

THUPT

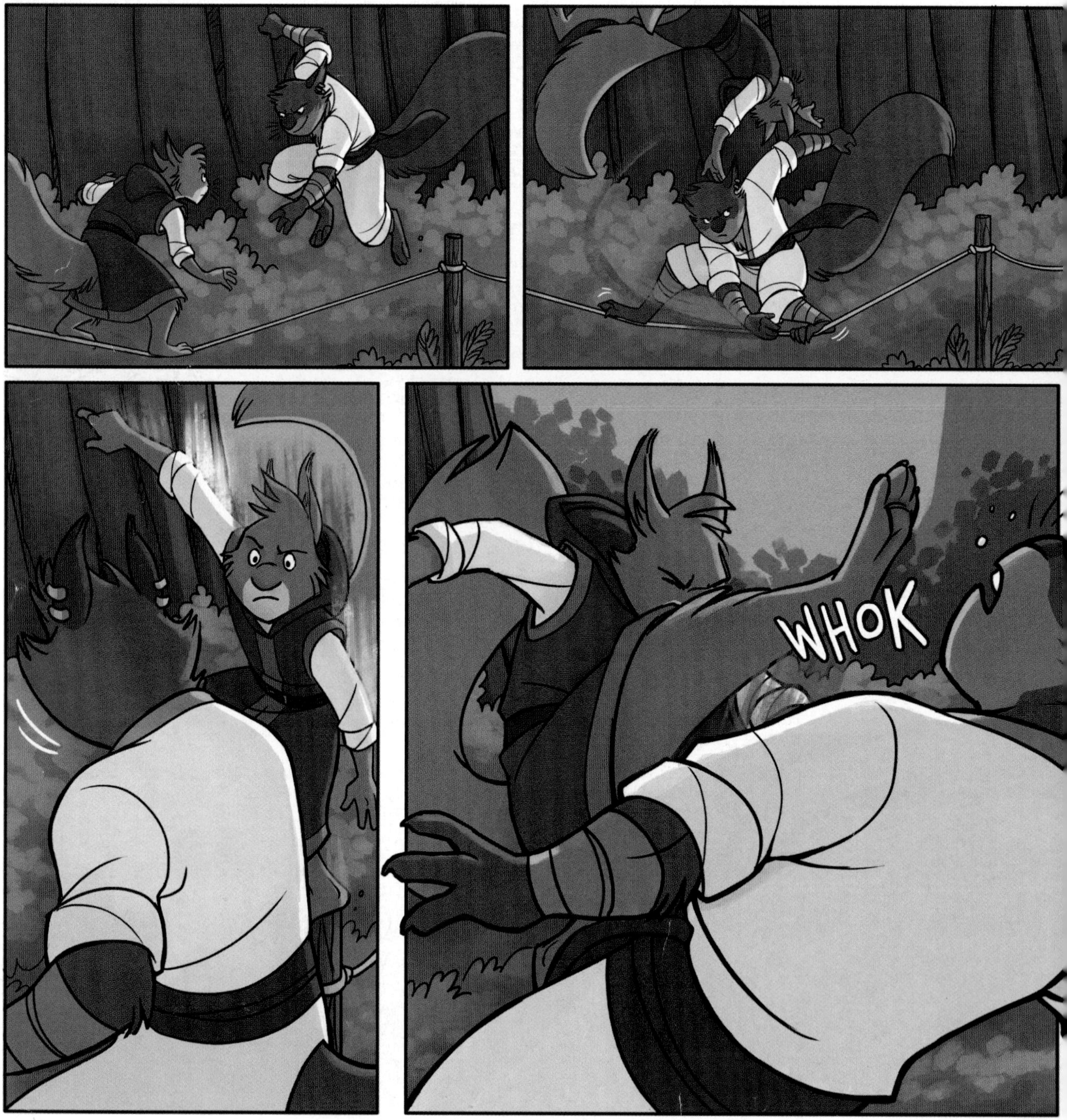
WHOK

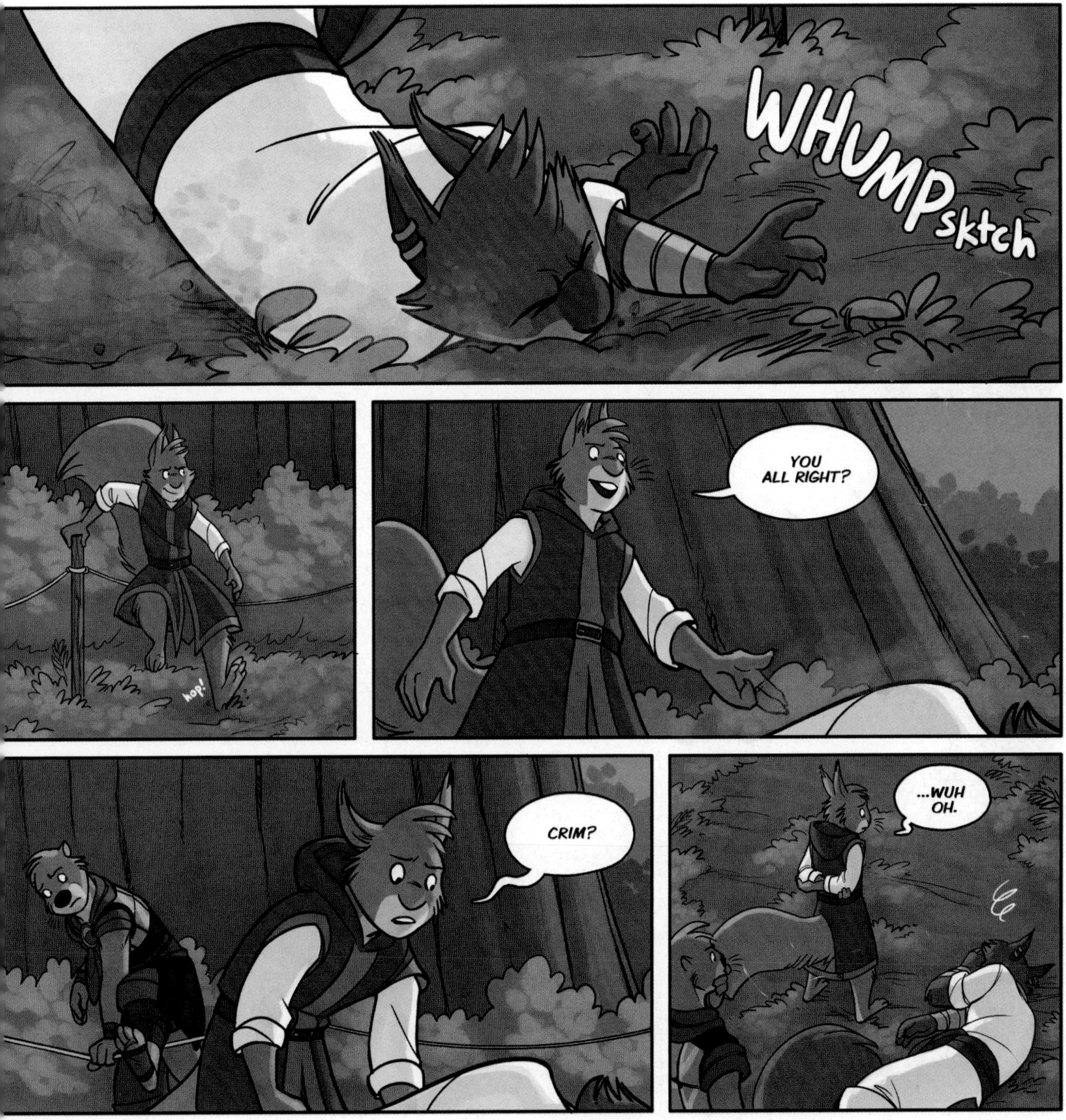
WHUMPsktch
hop!
YOU ALL RIGHT?
CRIM?
...WUH OH.

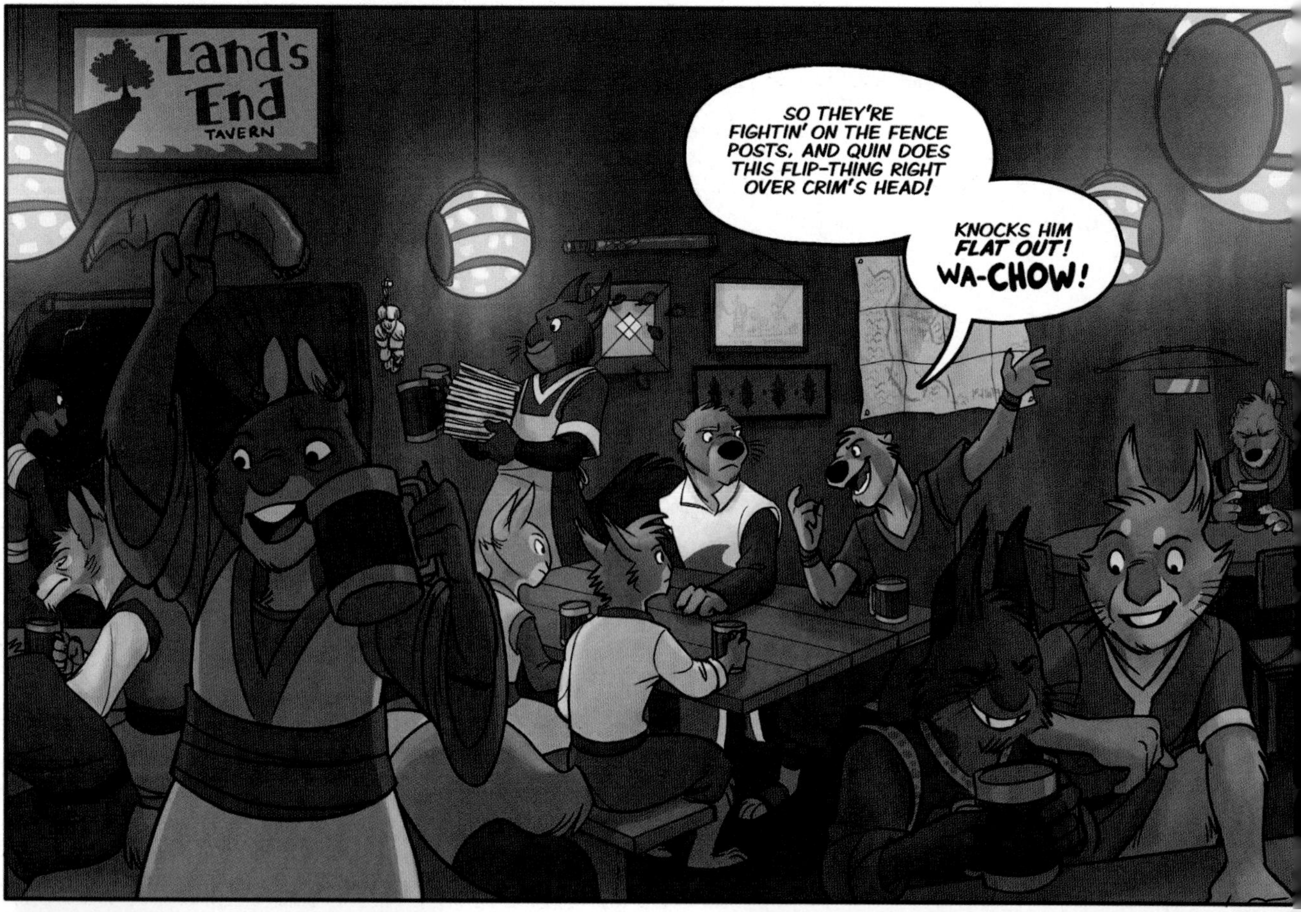
Land's End
TAVERN
SO THEY'RE FIGHTIN' ON THE FENCE POSTS, AND QUIN DOES THIS FLIP-THING RIGHT OVER CRIM'S HEAD!
KNOCKS HIM FLAT OUT! WA-CHOW!

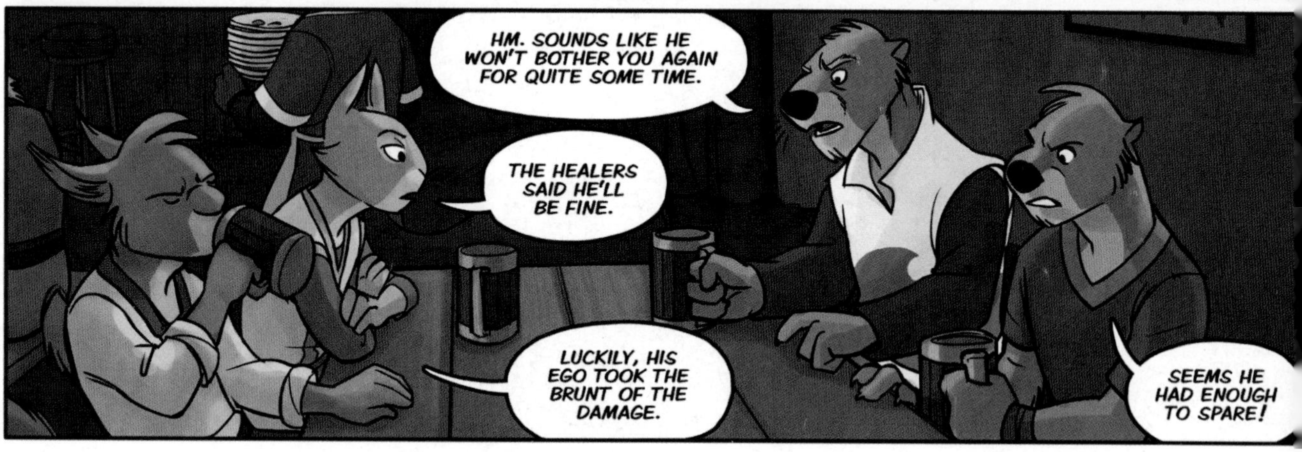
HM. SOUNDS LIKE HE WON'T BOTHER YOU AGAIN FOR QUITE SOME TIME.
THE HEALERS SAID HE'LL BE FINE.
LUCKILY, HIS EGO TOOK THE BRUNT OF THE DAMAGE.
SEEMS HE HAD ENOUGH TO SPARE!

WELL, HE'S ALWAYS BEEN THAT WAY.

IT JUST GOT A LOT WORSE WHEN HE WAS PASSED OVER FOR CAPTAINSHIP.

THE PLOT THICKENS.

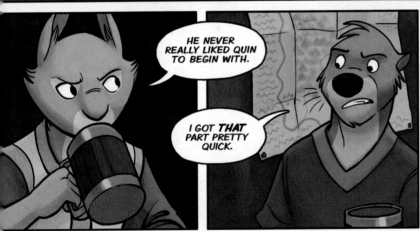

HE NEVER REALLY LIKED QUIN TO BEGIN WITH.

I GOT *THAT* PART PRETTY QUICK.

YEAH...

...SO!

HOW LONG DO YOU THINK YOU'LL BE GONE?

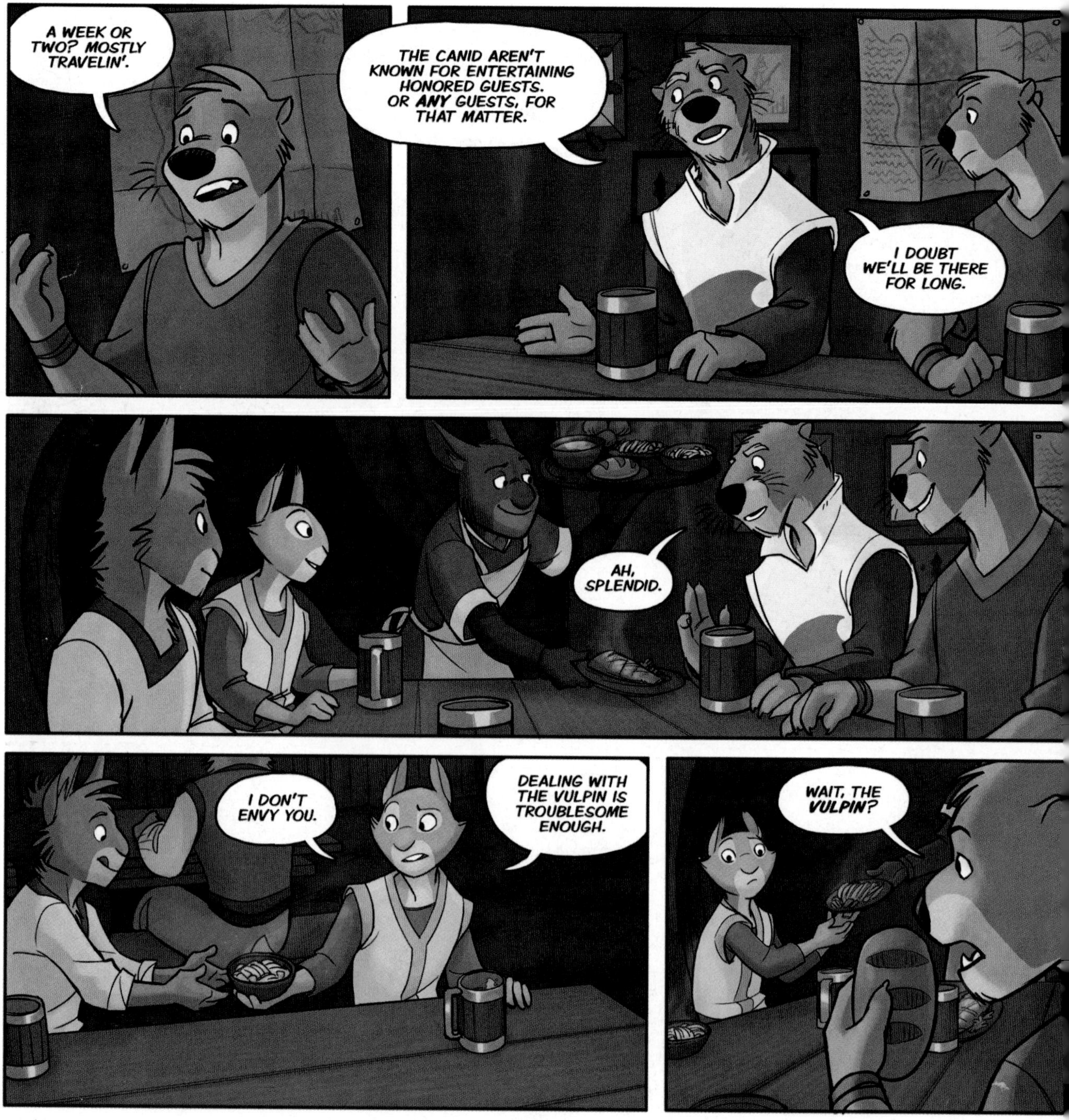
A WEEK OR TWO? MOSTLY TRAVELIN'.
THE CANID AREN'T KNOWN FOR ENTERTAINING HONORED GUESTS. OR **ANY** GUESTS, FOR THAT MATTER.
I DOUBT WE'LL BE THERE FOR LONG.
AH, SPLENDID.
I DON'T ENVY YOU.
DEALING WITH THE VULPIN IS TROUBLESOME ENOUGH.
WAIT, THE **VULPIN**?

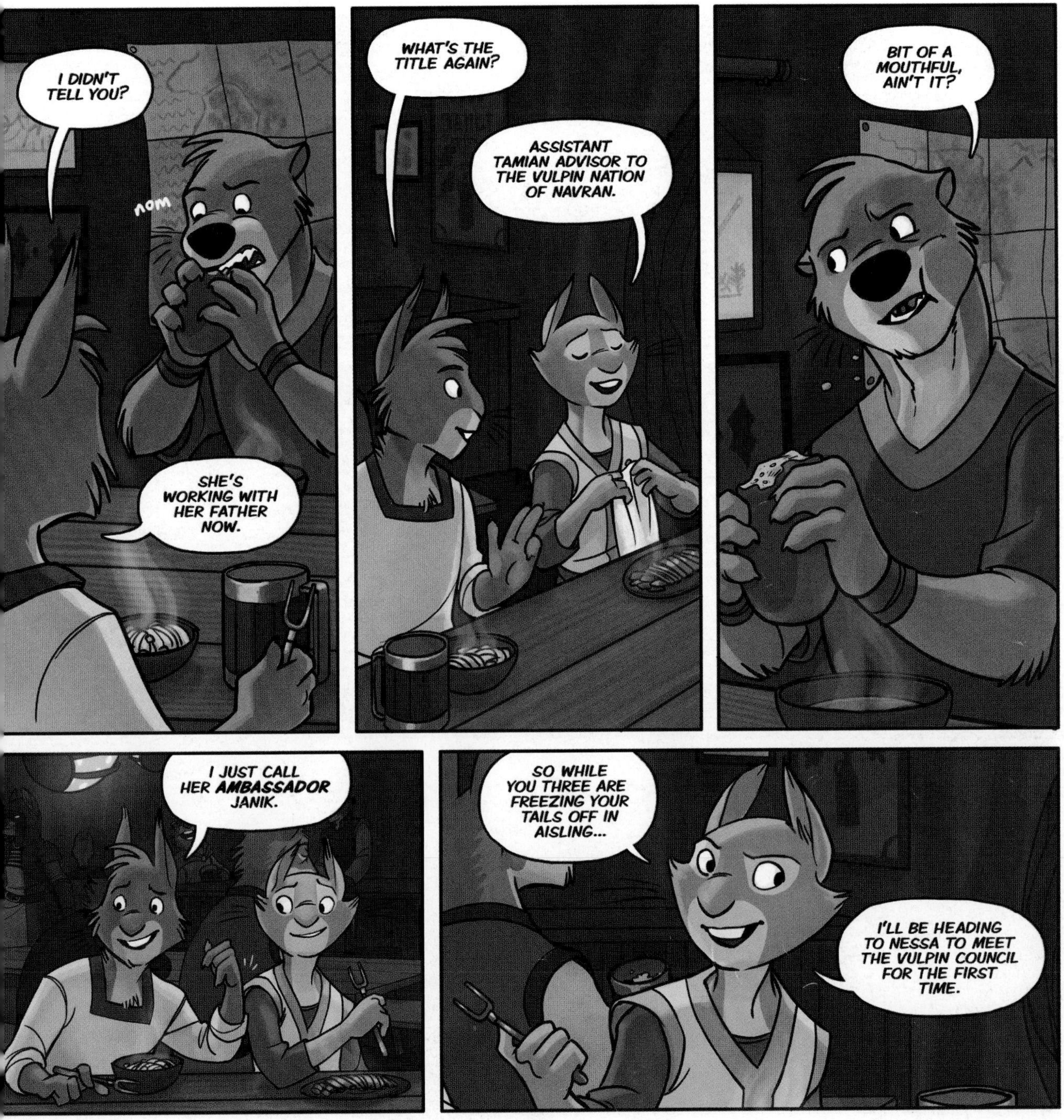
I DIDN'T TELL YOU?
nom
SHE'S WORKING WITH HER FATHER NOW.
WHAT'S THE TITLE AGAIN?
ASSISTANT TAMIAN ADVISOR TO THE VULPIN NATION OF NAVRAN.
BIT OF A MOUTHFUL, AIN'T IT?
I JUST CALL HER **AMBASSADOR** JANIK.
SO WHILE YOU THREE ARE FREEZING YOUR TAILS OFF IN AISLING...
I'LL BE HEADING TO NESSA TO MEET THE VULPIN COUNCIL FOR THE FIRST TIME.

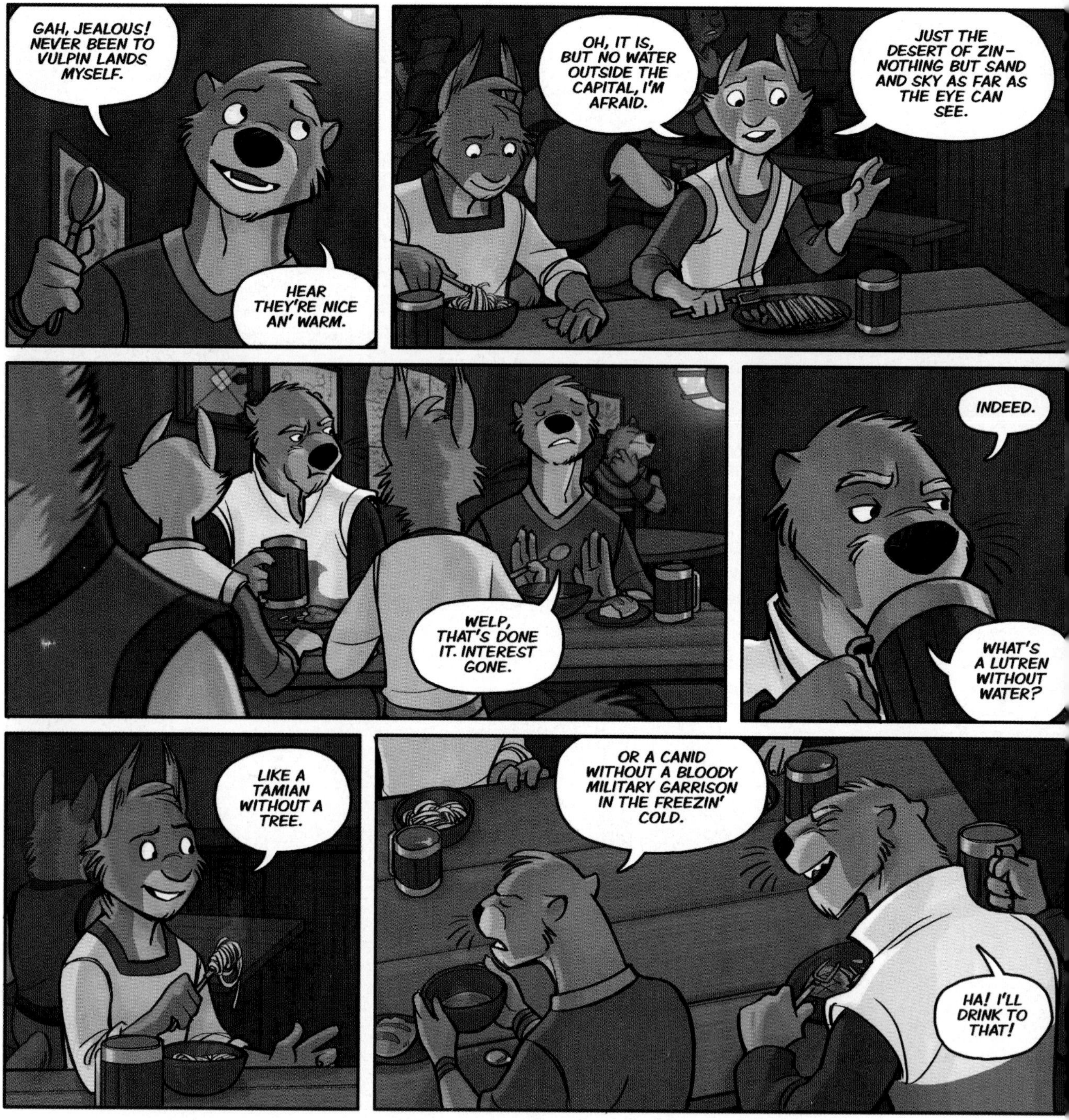
GAH, JEALOUS! NEVER BEEN TO VULPIN LANDS MYSELF.
HEAR THEY'RE NICE AN' WARM.
OH, IT IS, BUT NO WATER OUTSIDE THE CAPITAL, I'M AFRAID.
JUST THE DESERT OF ZIN– NOTHING BUT SAND AND SKY AS FAR AS THE EYE CAN SEE.
WELP, THAT'S DONE IT. INTEREST GONE.
INDEED.
WHAT'S A LUTREN WITHOUT WATER?
LIKE A TAMIAN WITHOUT A TREE.
OR A CANID WITHOUT A BLOODY MILITARY GARRISON IN THE FREEZIN' COLD.
HA! I'LL DRINK TO THAT!

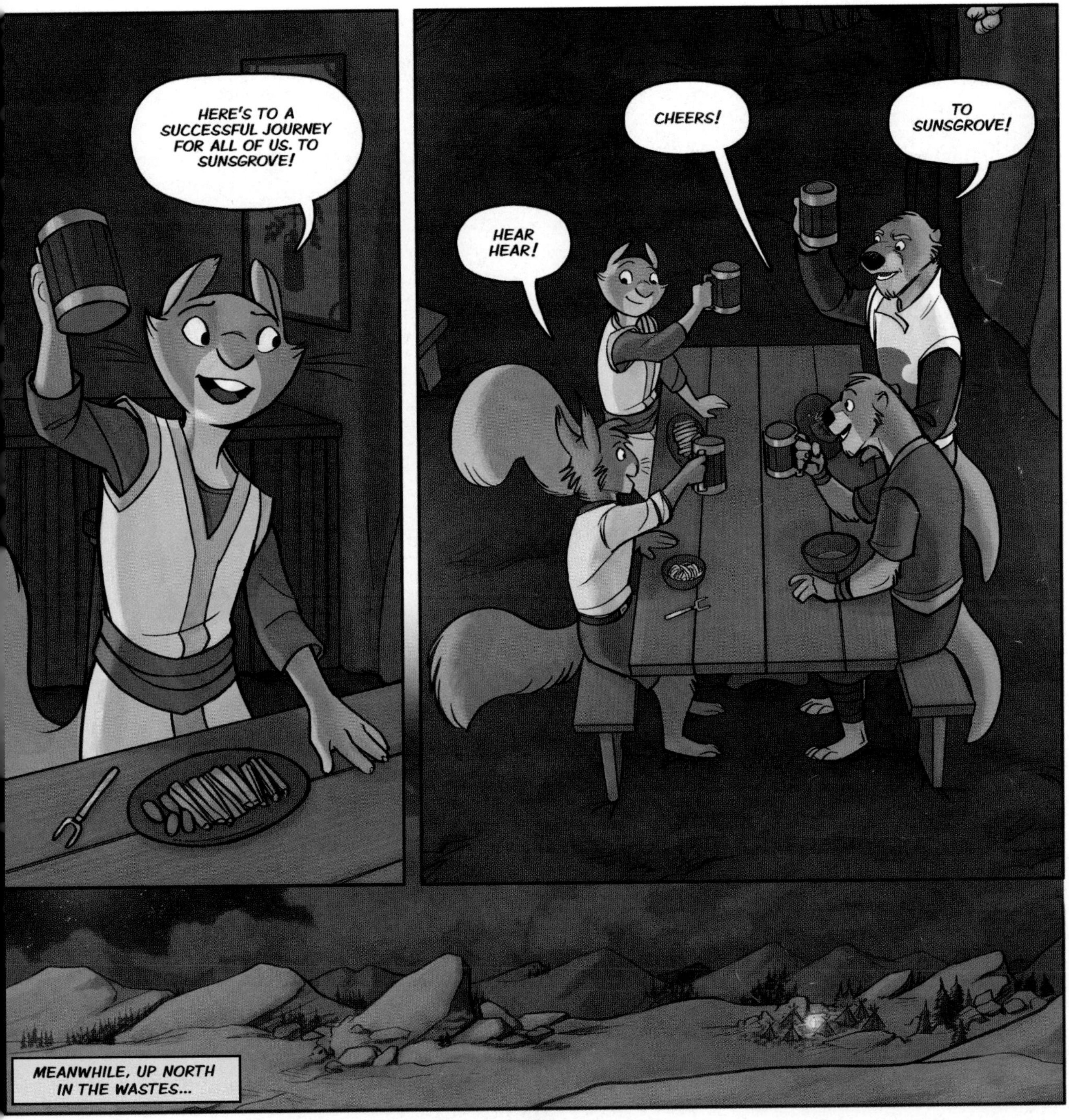
HERE'S TO A SUCCESSFUL JOURNEY FOR ALL OF US. TO SUNSGROVE!
HEAR HEAR!
CHEERS!
TO SUNSGROVE!
MEANWHILE, UP NORTH IN THE WASTES...

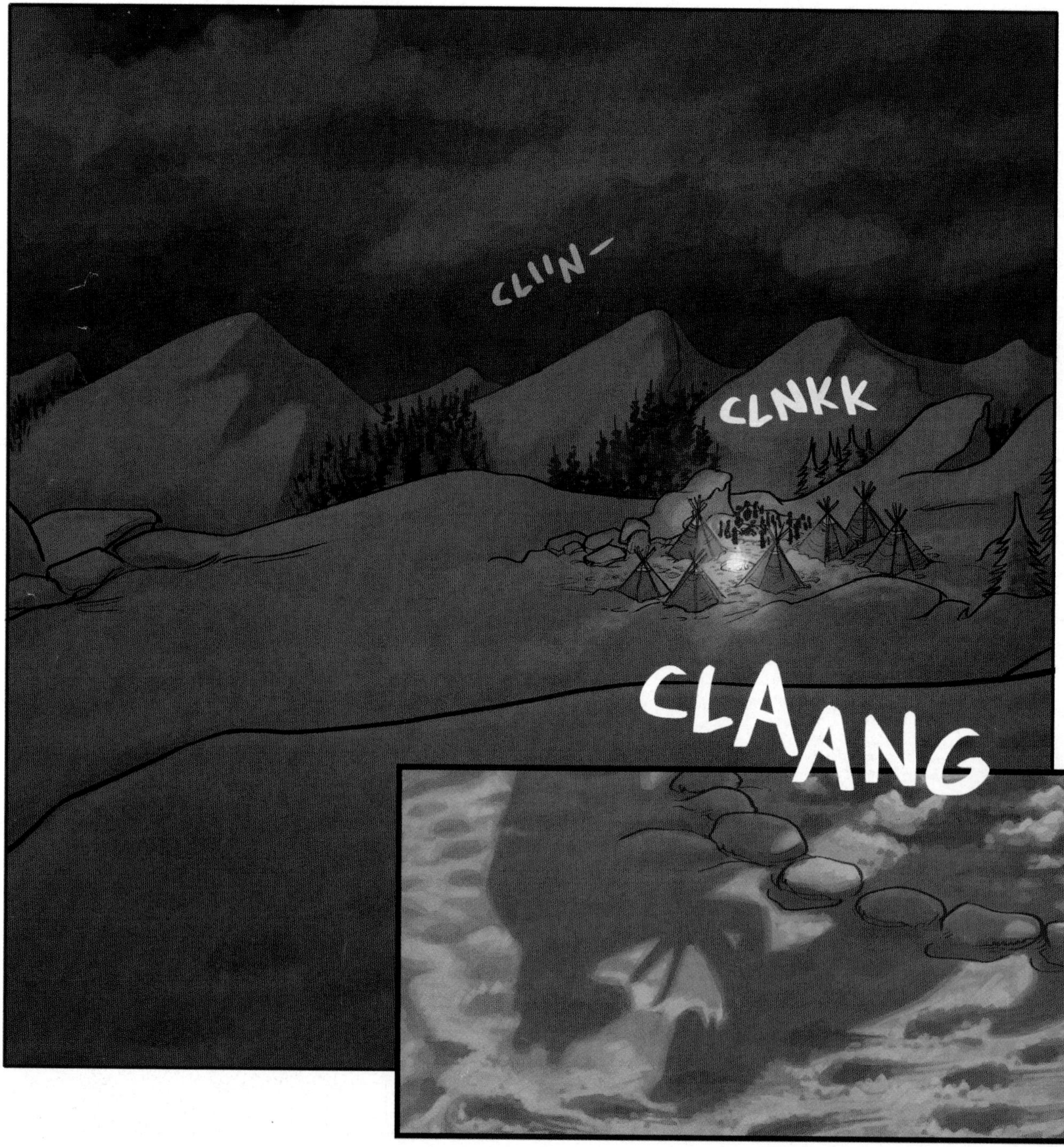
CLIIN-
CLNKK
CLAANG

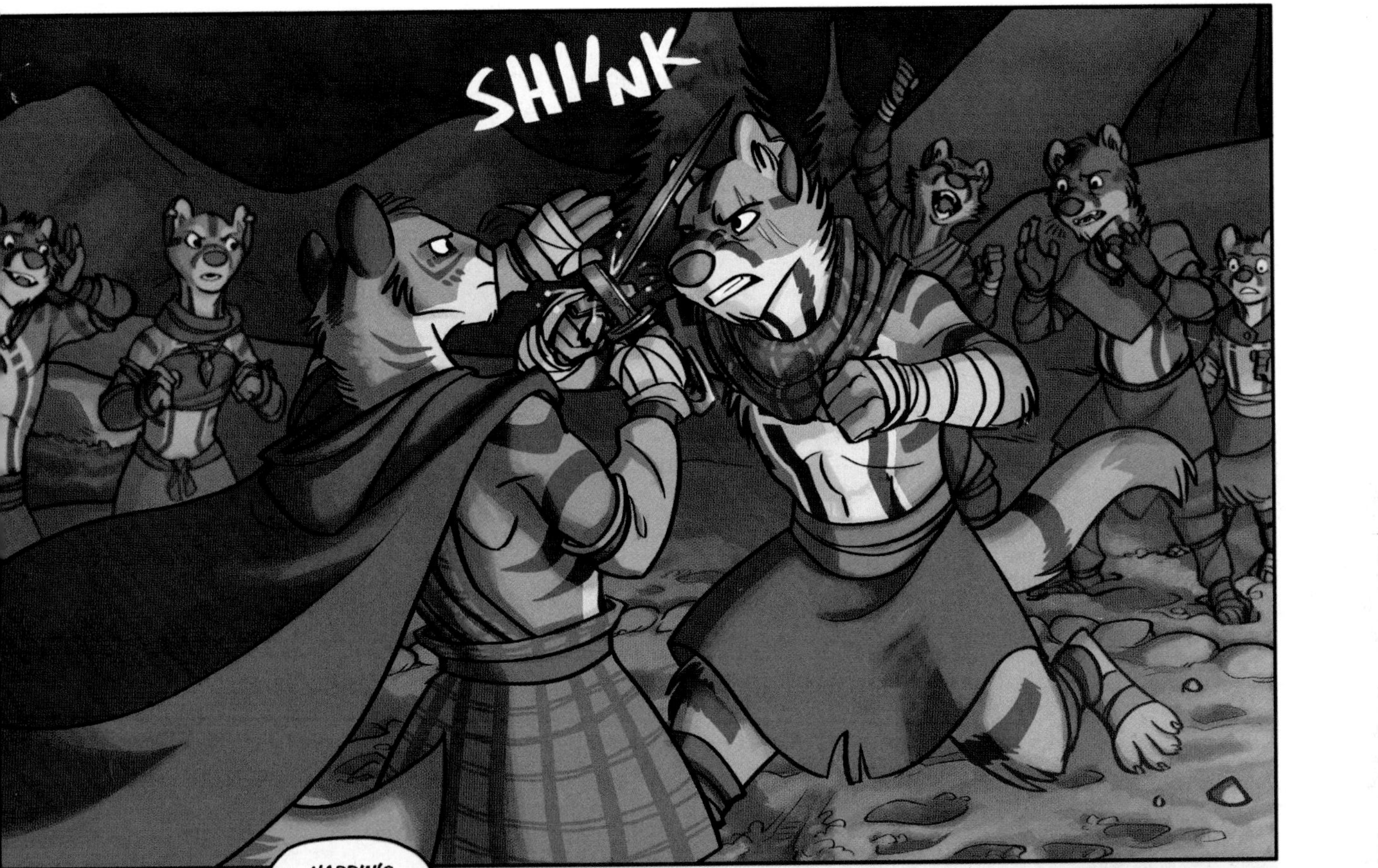
SHI'NK

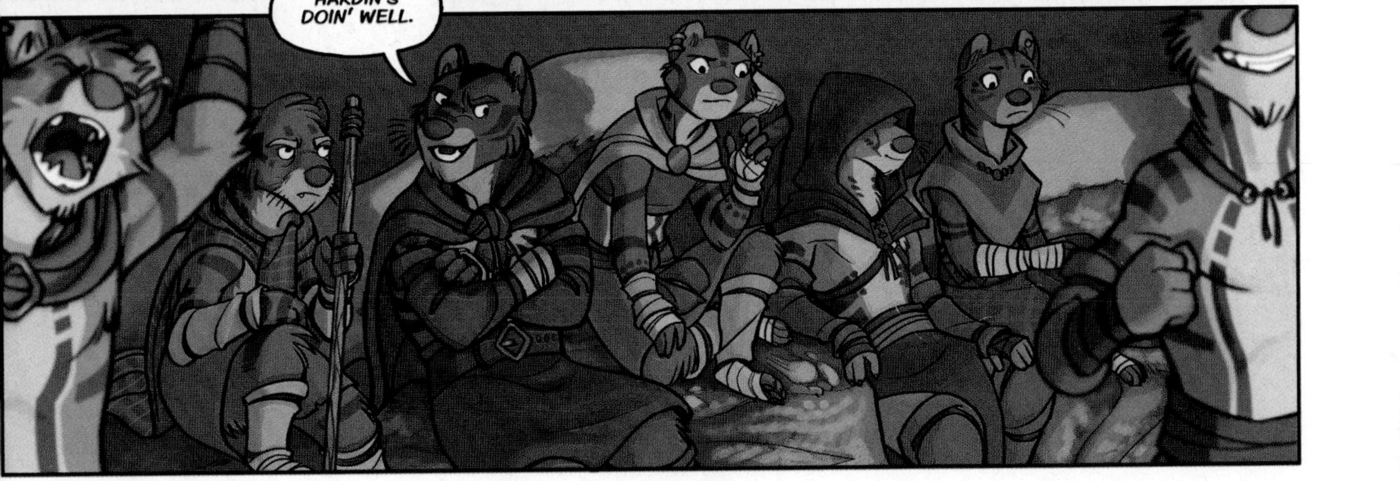
HARDIN'S DOIN' WELL.

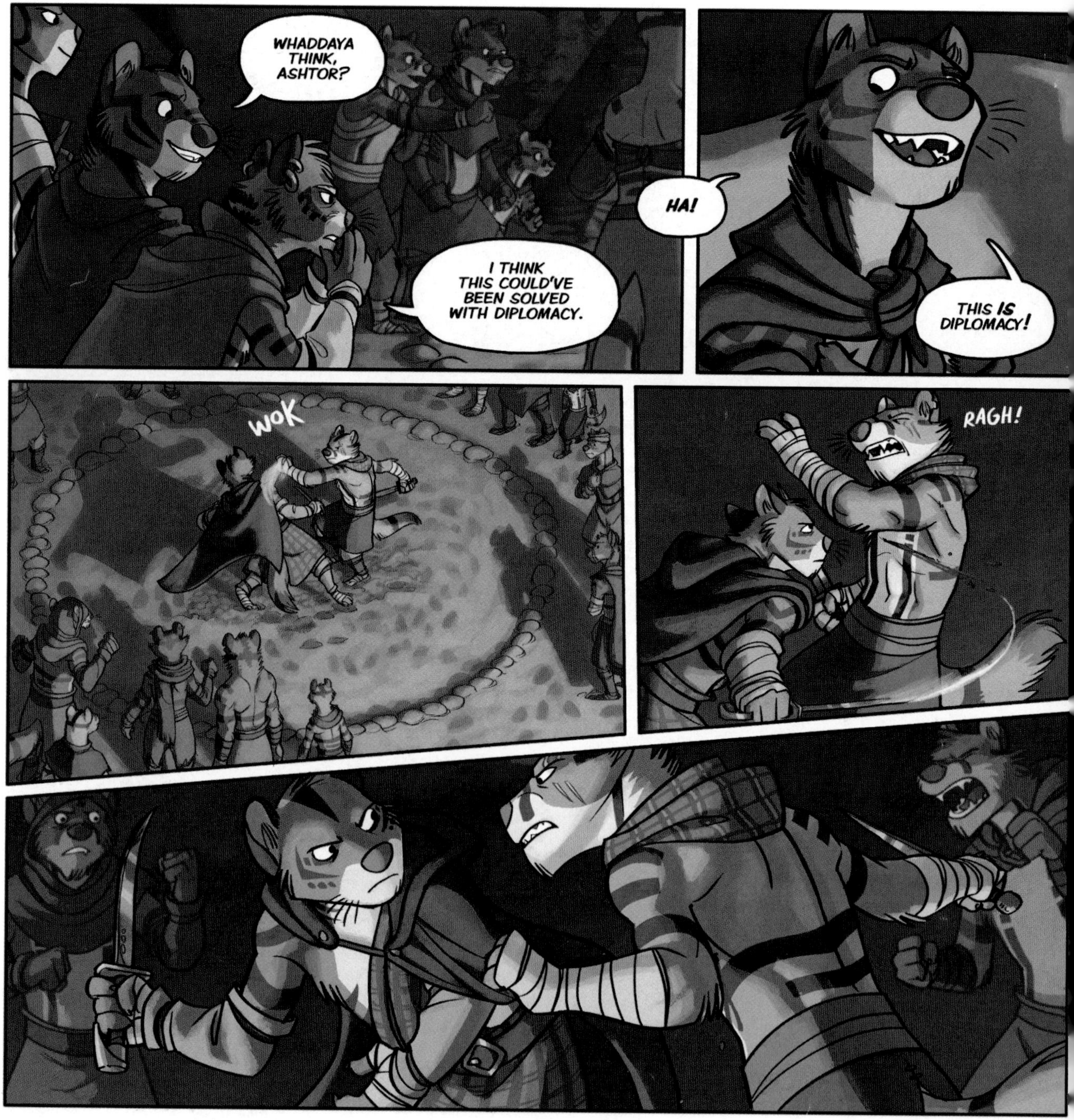
WHADDAYA THINK, ASHTOR?
I THINK THIS COULD'VE BEEN SOLVED WITH DIPLOMACY.
HA!
THIS IS DIPLOMACY!
WOK
RAGH!

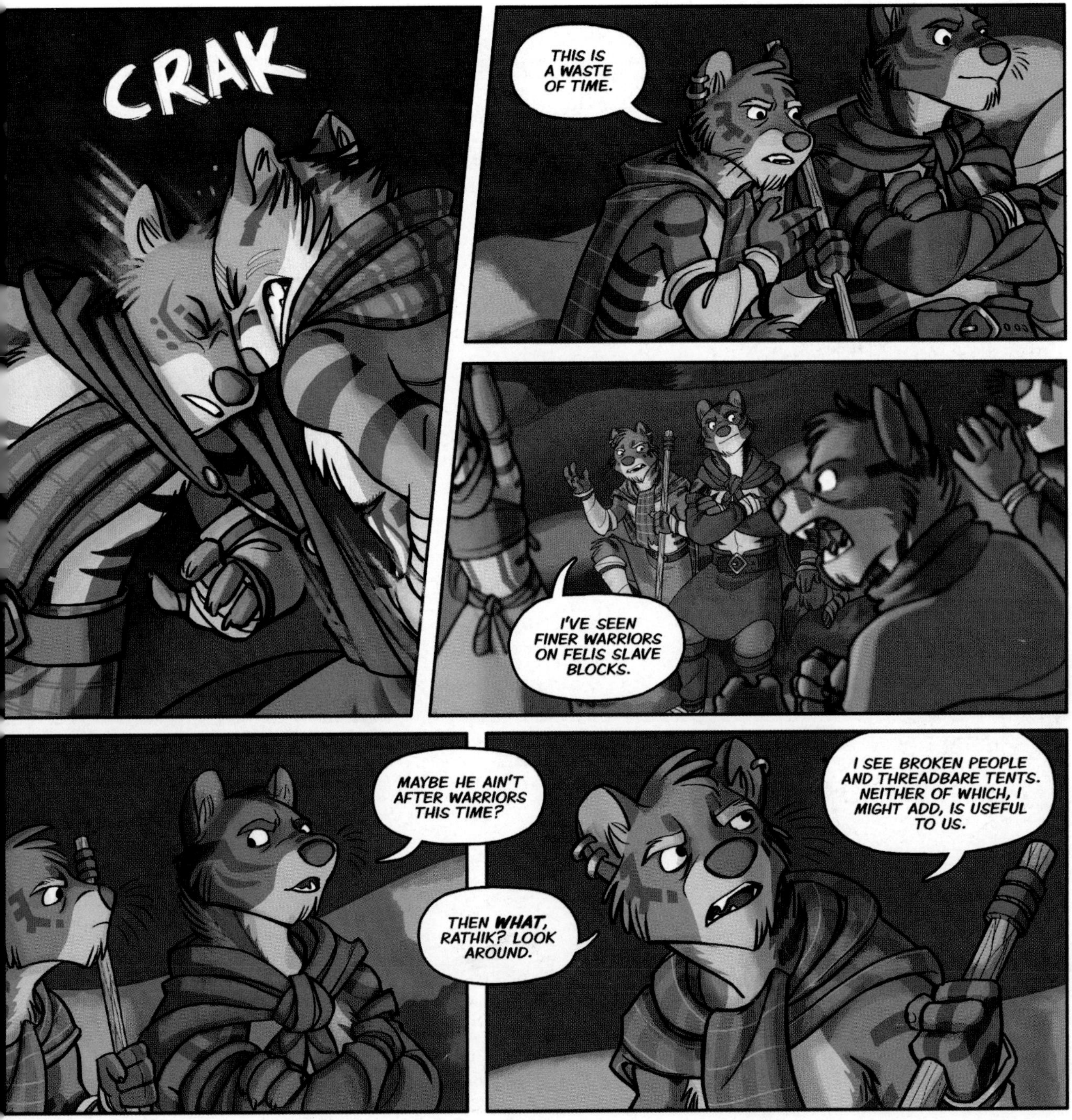
CRAK
THIS IS A WASTE OF TIME.
I'VE SEEN FINER WARRIORS ON FELIS SLAVE BLOCKS.
MAYBE HE AIN'T AFTER WARRIORS THIS TIME?
THEN **WHAT**, RATHIK? LOOK AROUND.
I SEE BROKEN PEOPLE AND THREADBARE TENTS. NEITHER OF WHICH, I MIGHT ADD, IS USEFUL TO US.

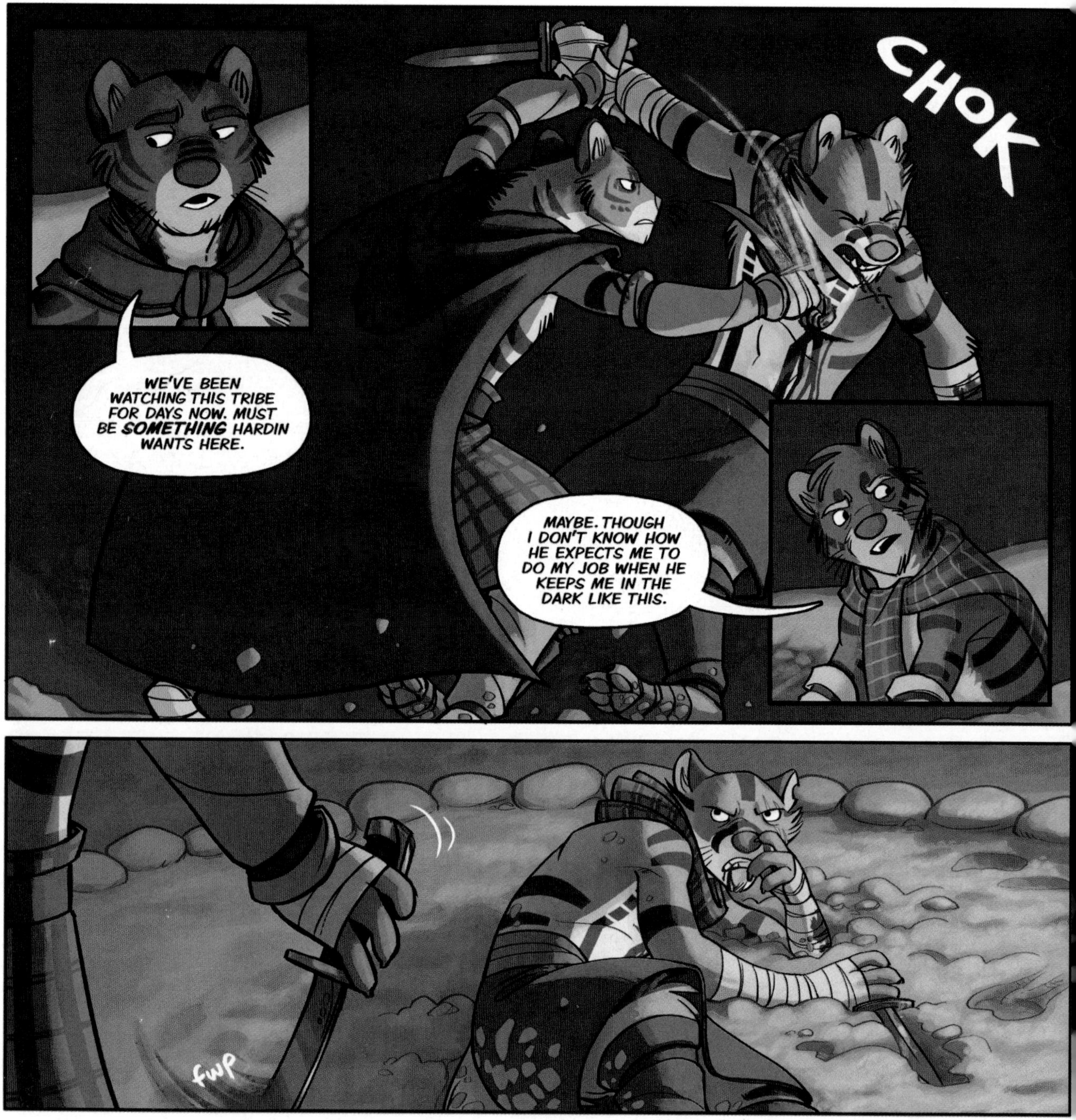
CHOK
WE'VE BEEN WATCHING THIS TRIBE FOR DAYS NOW. MUST BE SOMETHING HARDIN WANTS HERE.
MAYBE. THOUGH I DON'T KNOW HOW HE EXPECTS ME TO DO MY JOB WHEN HE KEEPS ME IN THE DARK LIKE THIS.
fwp

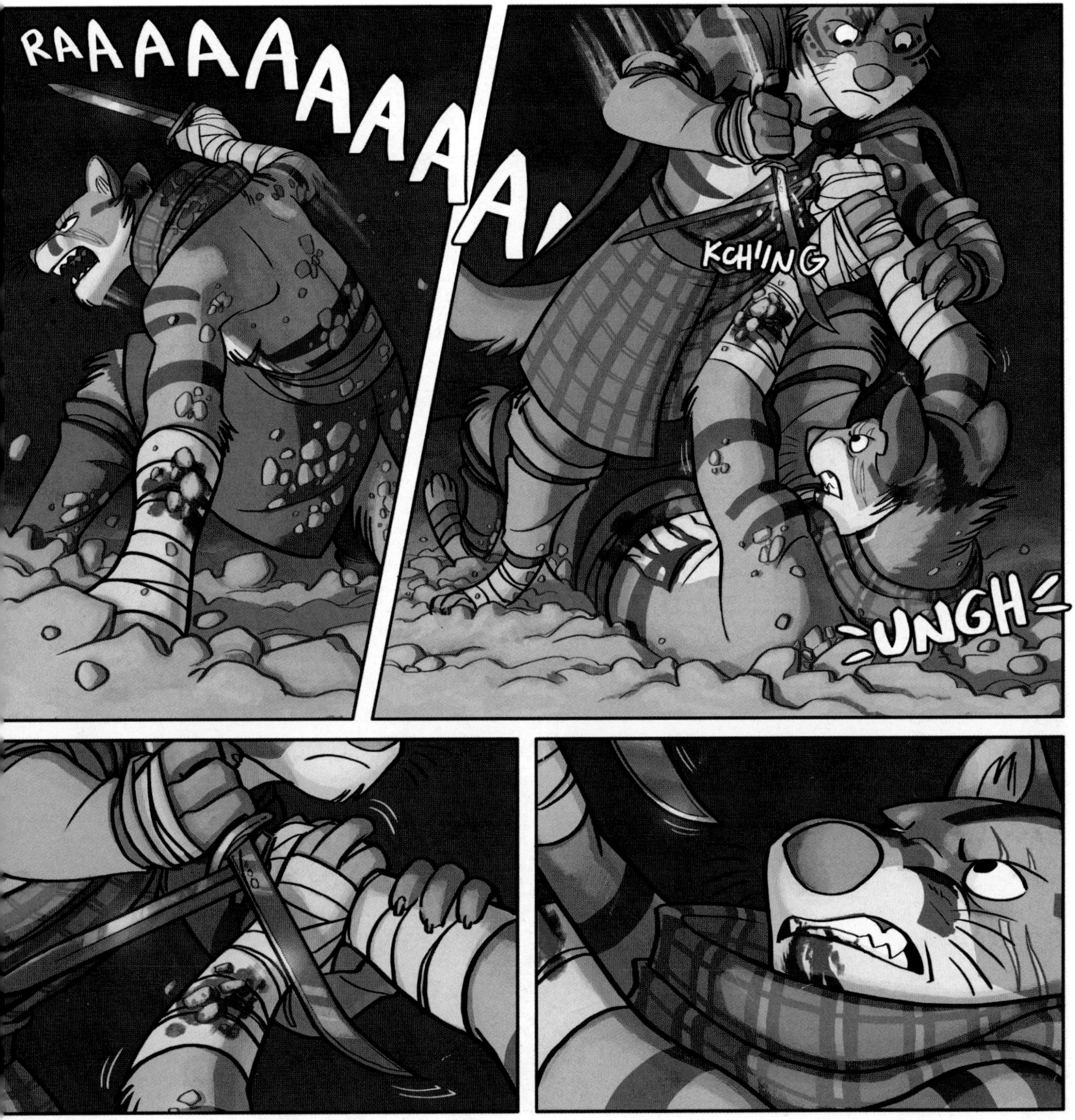
RAAAAAAAAAAAA
KCHIING
UNGH

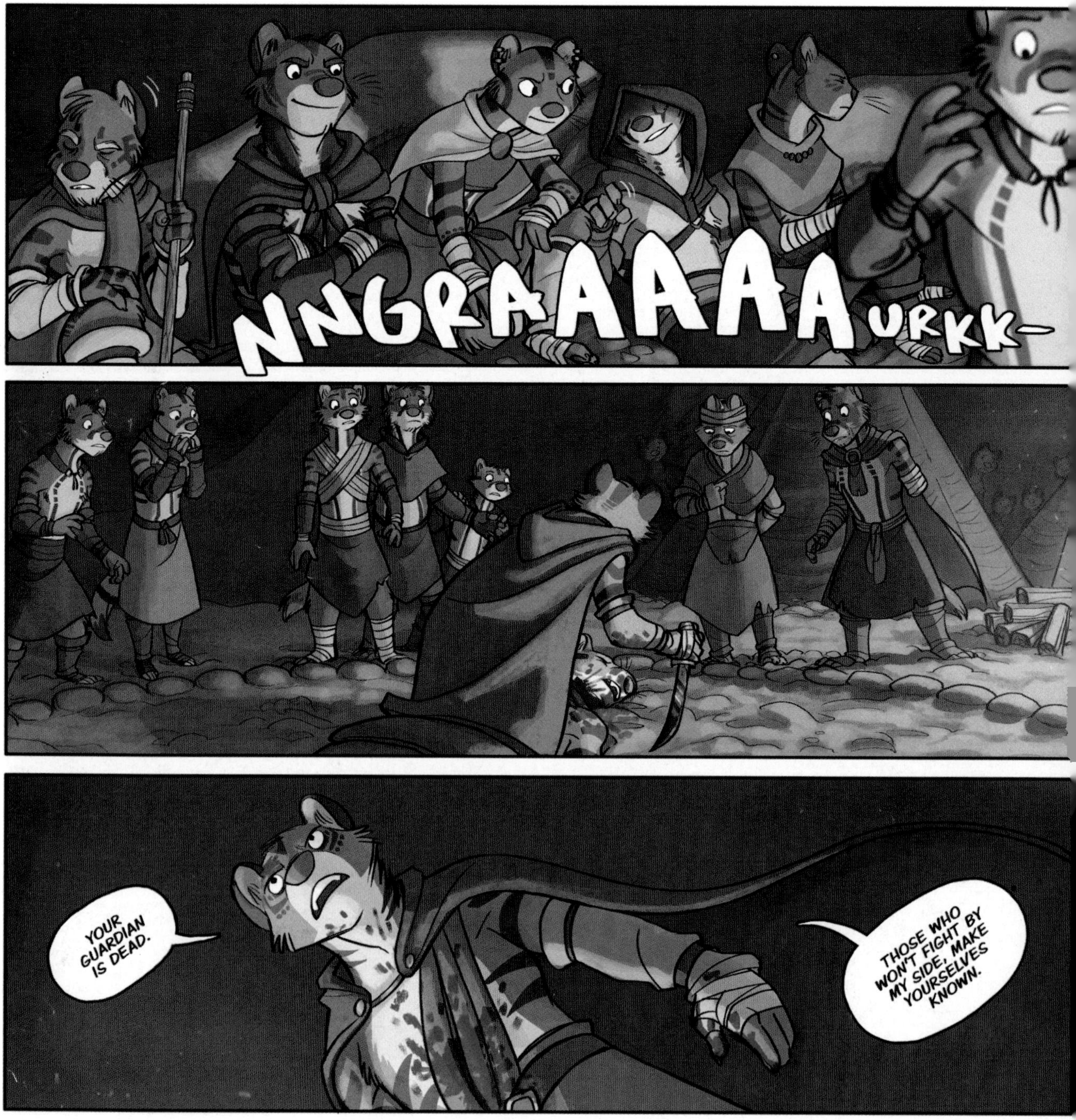
NNGRAAAAAAURKK-
YOUR GUARDIAN IS DEAD.
THOSE WHO WON'T FIGHT BY MY SIDE, MAKE YOURSELVES KNOWN.

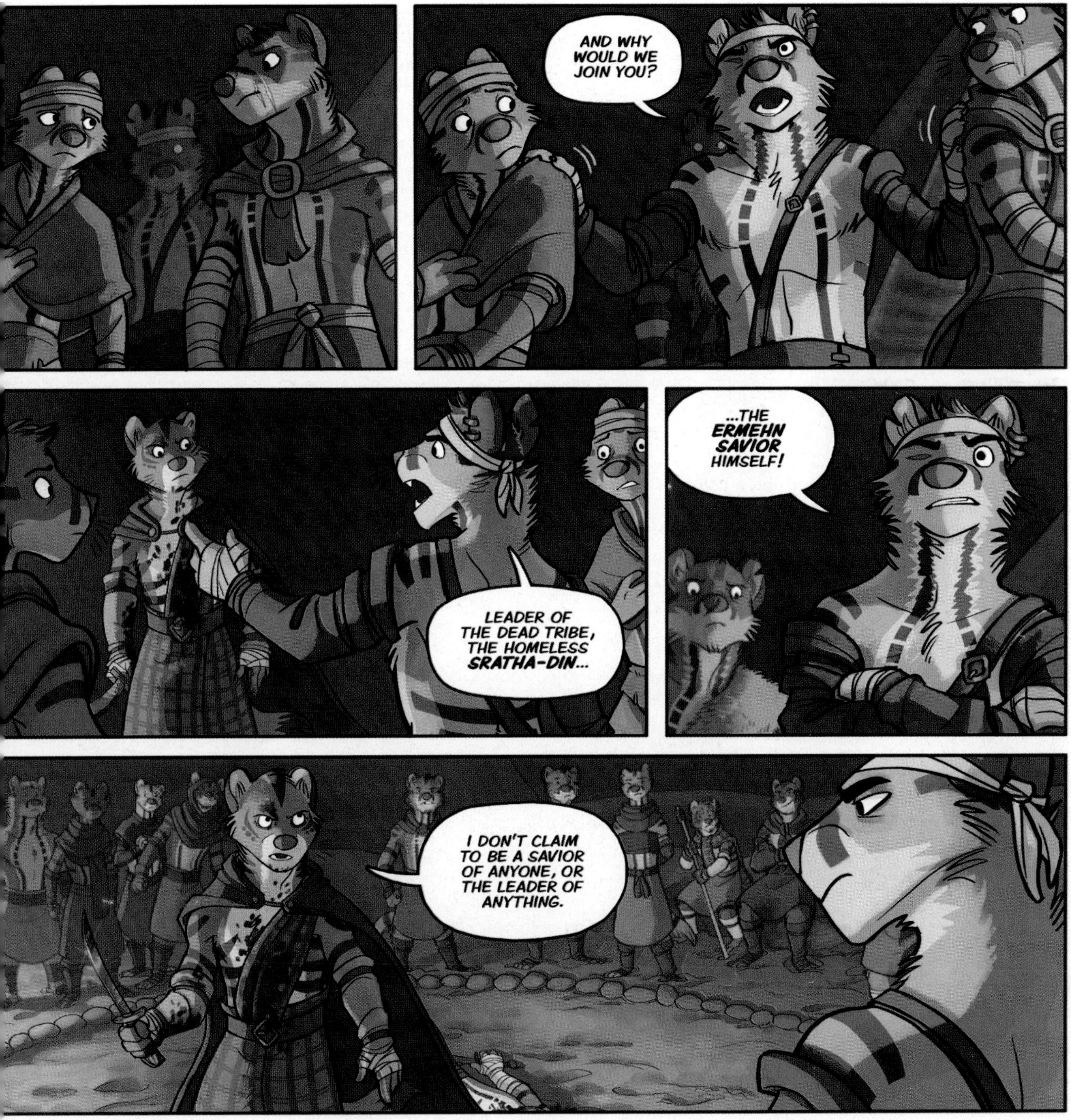
AND WHY WOULD WE JOIN YOU?
LEADER OF THE DEAD TRIBE, THE HOMELESS SRATHA-DIN...
...THE ERMEHN SAVIOR HIMSELF!
I DON'T CLAIM TO BE A SAVIOR OF ANYONE, OR THE LEADER OF ANYTHING.

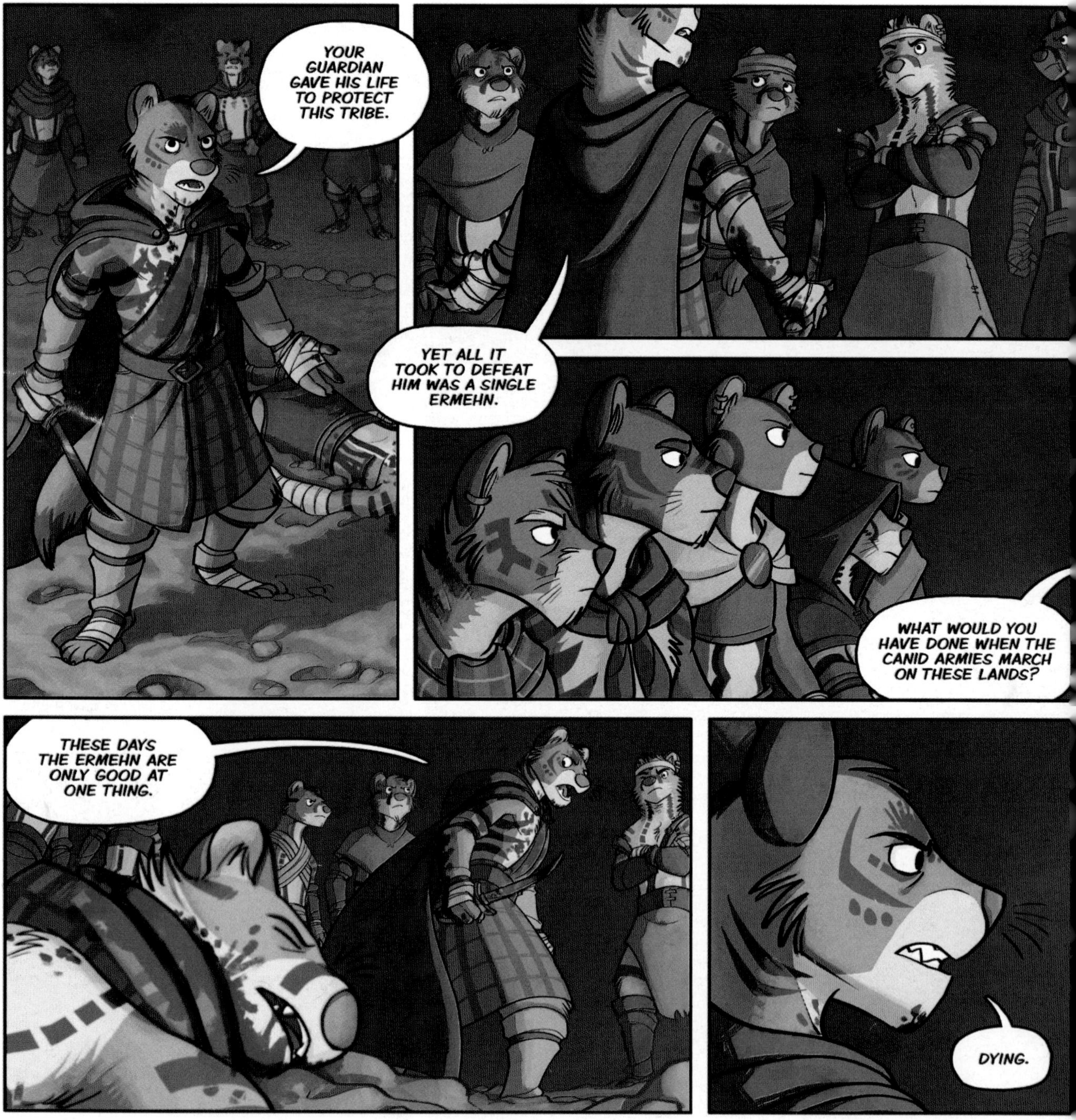
YOUR GUARDIAN GAVE HIS LIFE TO PROTECT THIS TRIBE.
YET ALL IT TOOK TO DEFEAT HIM WAS A SINGLE ERMEHN.
WHAT WOULD YOU HAVE DONE WHEN THE CANID ARMIES MARCH ON THESE LANDS?
THESE DAYS THE ERMEHN ARE ONLY GOOD AT ONE THING.
DYING.

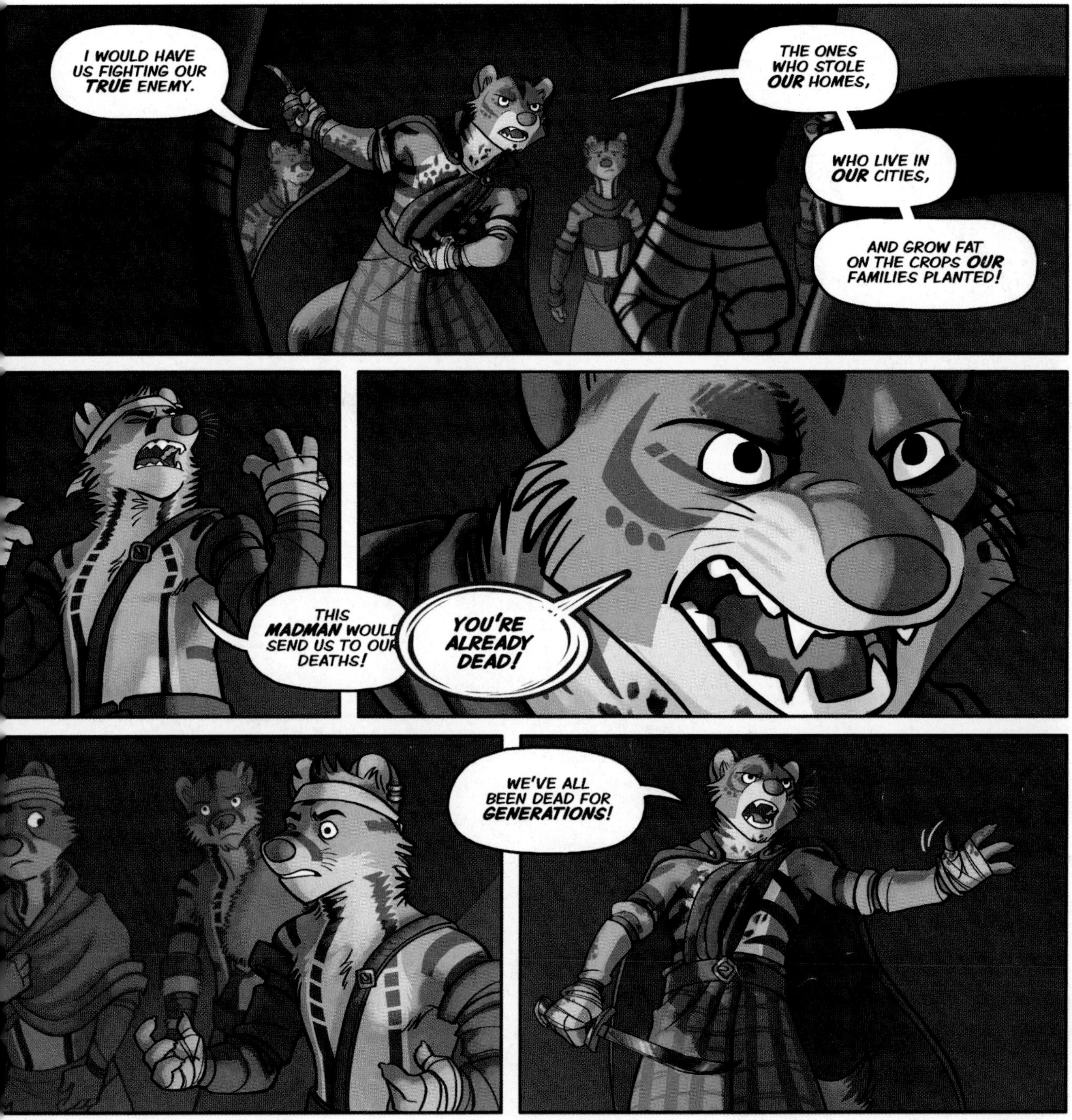
I WOULD HAVE US FIGHTING OUR TRUE ENEMY.
THE ONES WHO STOLE OUR HOMES,
WHO LIVE IN OUR CITIES,
AND GROW FAT ON THE CROPS OUR FAMILIES PLANTED!
THIS MADMAN WOULD SEND US TO OUR DEATHS!
YOU'RE ALREADY DEAD!
WE'VE ALL BEEN DEAD FOR GENERATIONS!

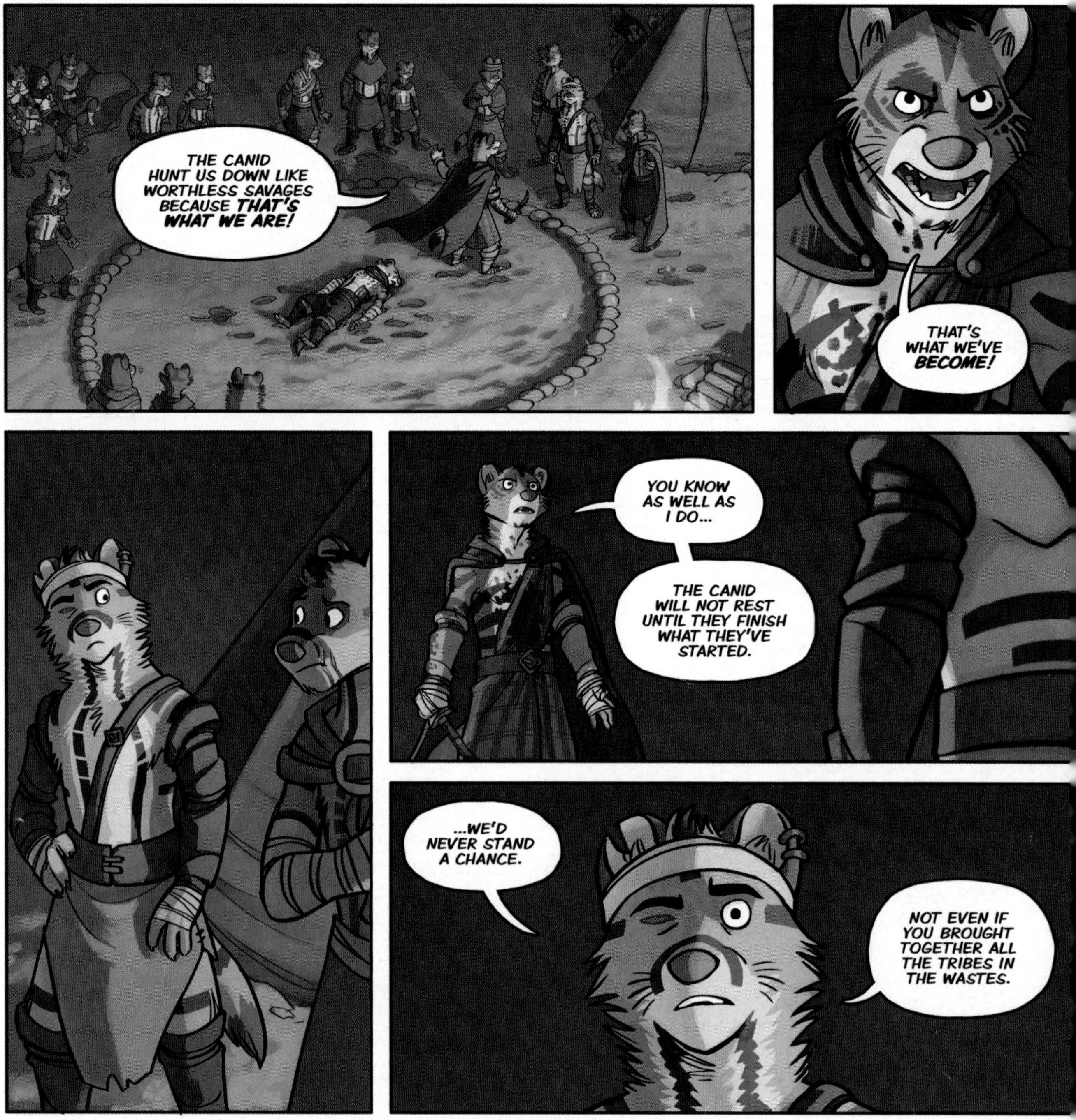
THE CANID HUNT US DOWN LIKE WORTHLESS SAVAGES BECAUSE THAT'S WHAT WE ARE!
THAT'S WHAT WE'VE BECOME!
YOU KNOW AS WELL AS I DO...
THE CANID WILL NOT REST UNTIL THEY FINISH WHAT THEY'VE STARTED.
...WE'D NEVER STAND A CHANCE.
NOT EVEN IF YOU BROUGHT TOGETHER ALL THE TRIBES IN THE WASTES.

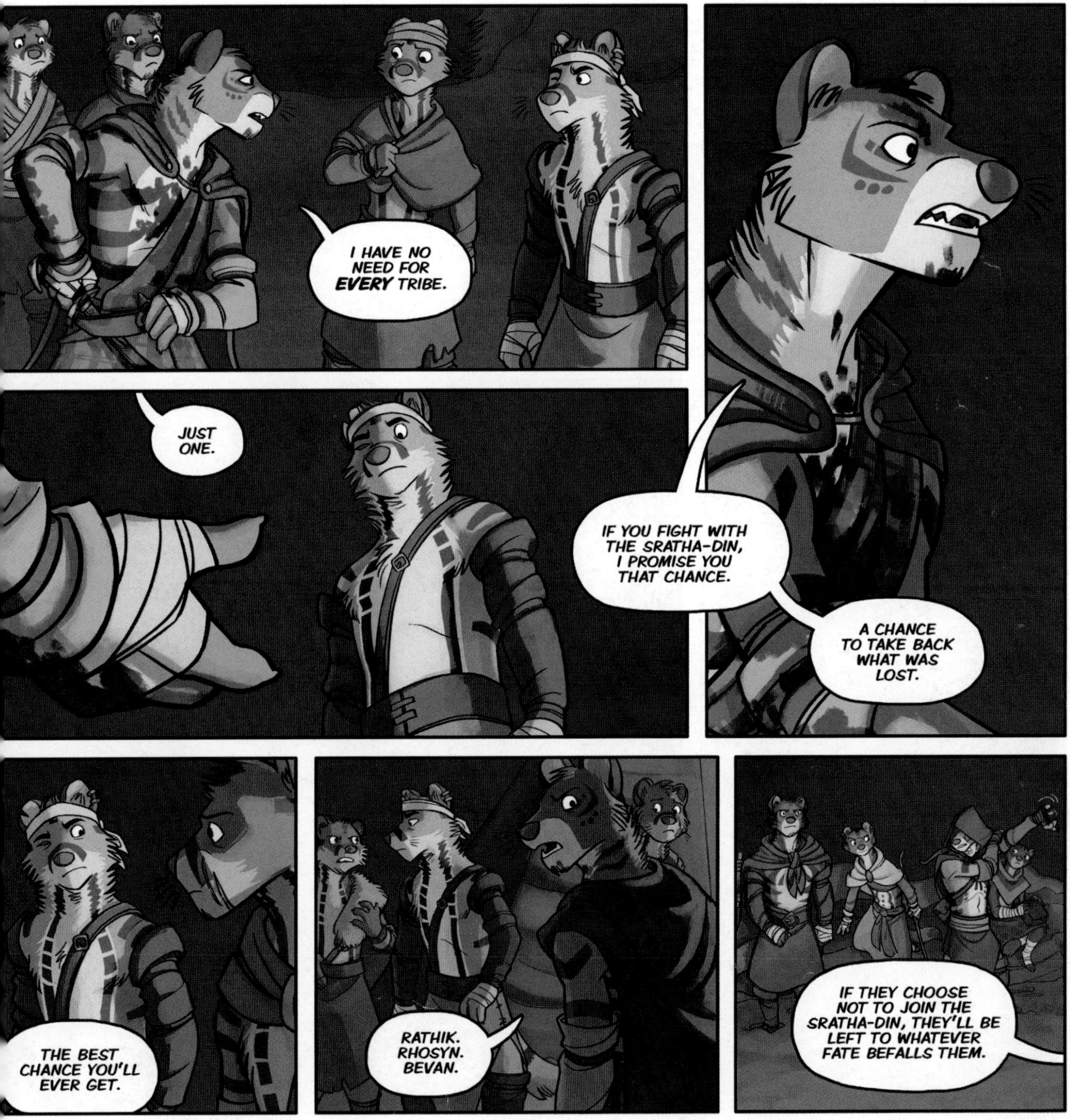
I HAVE NO NEED FOR EVERY TRIBE.
JUST ONE.
IF YOU FIGHT WITH THE SRATHA-DIN, I PROMISE YOU THAT CHANCE.
A CHANCE TO TAKE BACK WHAT WAS LOST.
THE BEST CHANCE YOU'LL EVER GET.
RATHIK. RHOSYN. BEVAN.
IF THEY CHOOSE NOT TO JOIN THE SRATHA-DIN, THEY'LL BE LEFT TO WHATEVER FATE BEFALLS THEM.

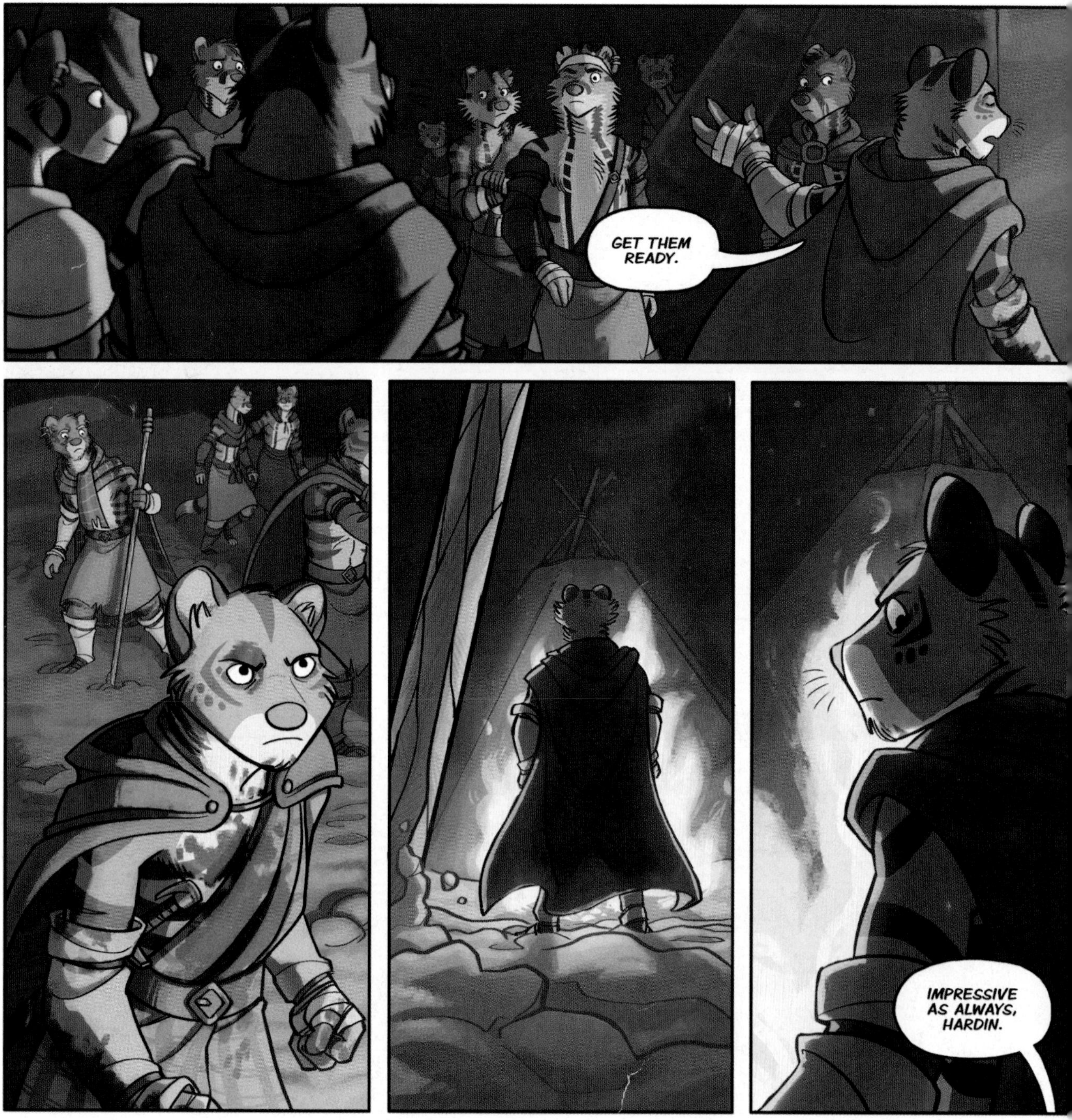
GET THEM READY.
IMPRESSIVE AS ALWAYS, HARDIN.

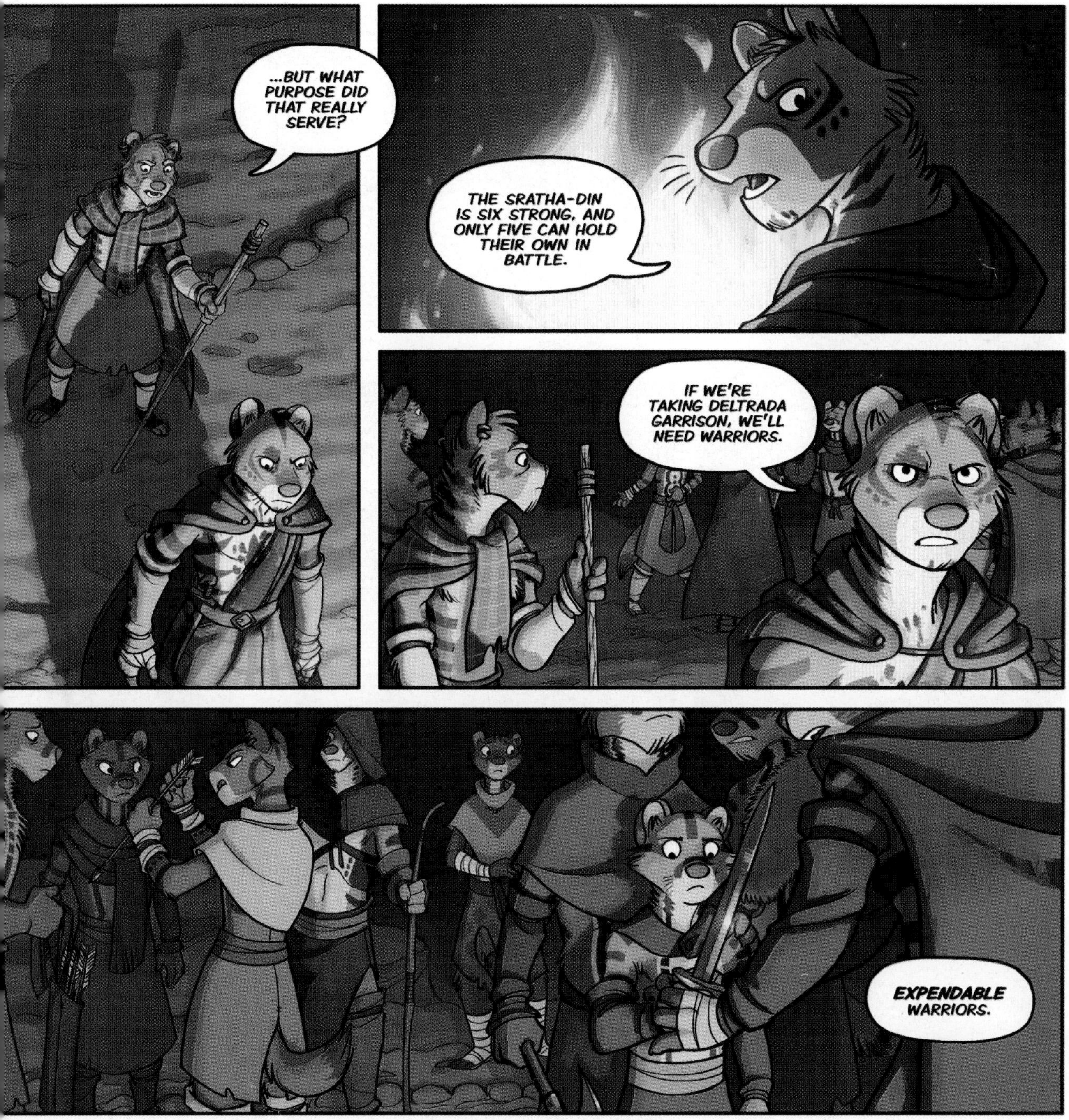
...BUT WHAT PURPOSE DID THAT REALLY SERVE?
THE SRATHA-DIN IS SIX STRONG, AND ONLY FIVE CAN HOLD THEIR OWN IN BATTLE.
IF WE'RE TAKING DELTRADA GARRISON, WE'LL NEED WARRIORS.
EXPENDABLE WARRIORS.

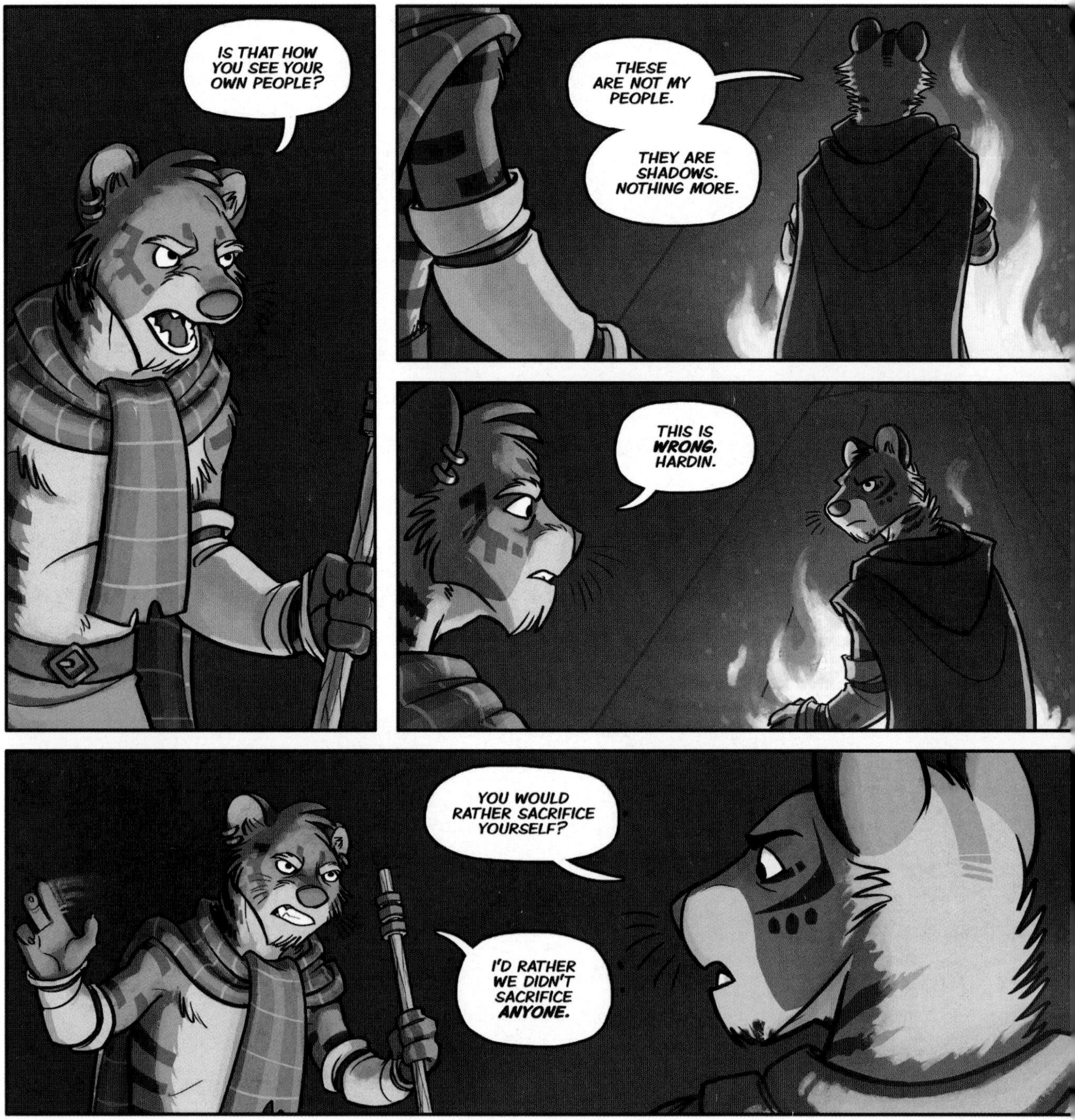
IS THAT HOW YOU SEE YOUR OWN PEOPLE?
THESE ARE NOT MY PEOPLE.
THEY ARE SHADOWS. NOTHING MORE.
THIS IS **WRONG,** HARDIN.
YOU WOULD RATHER SACRIFICE YOURSELF?
I'D RATHER WE DIDN'T SACRIFICE **ANYONE.**

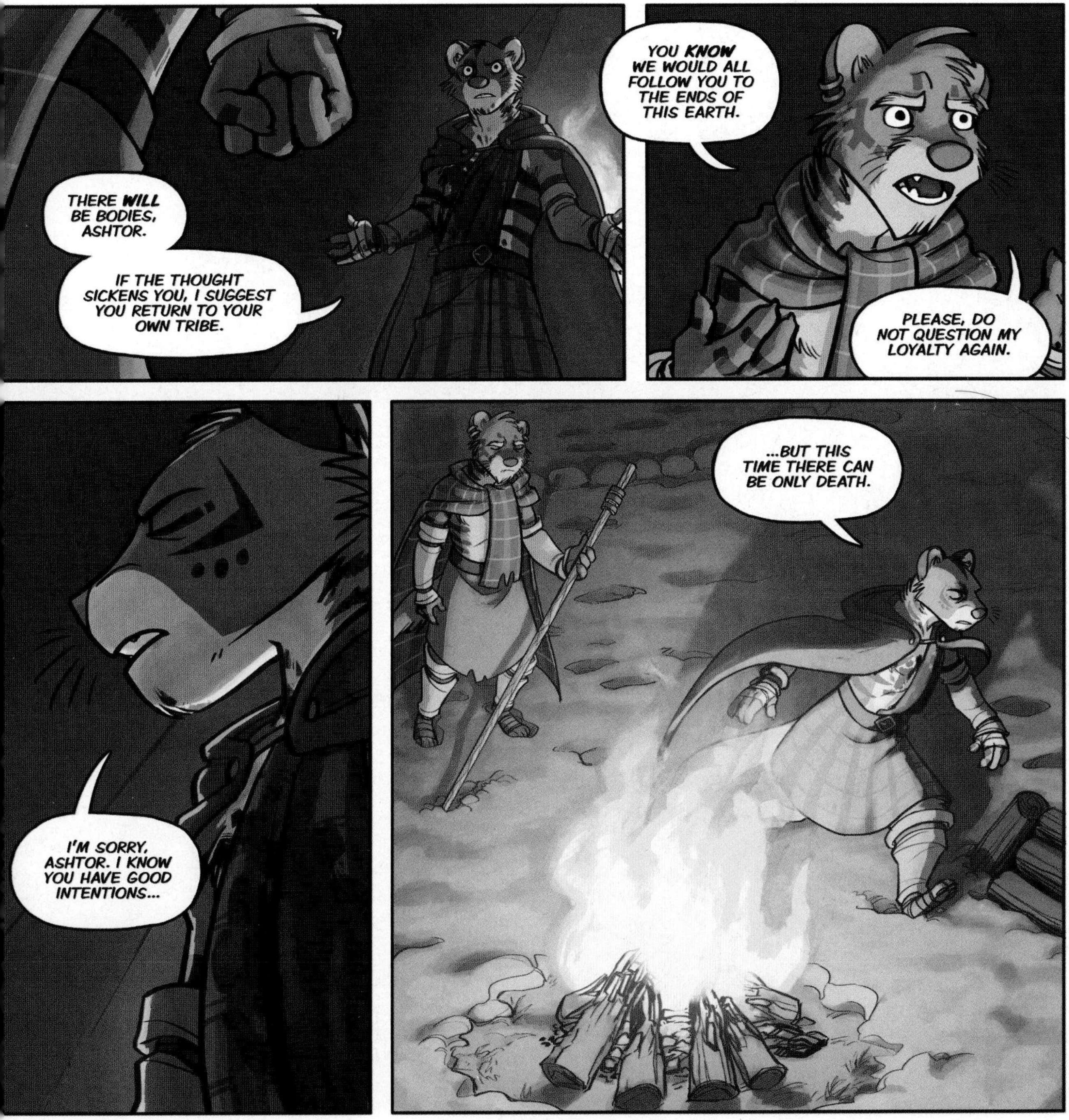
THERE WILL BE BODIES, ASHTOR.
IF THE THOUGHT SICKENS YOU, I SUGGEST YOU RETURN TO YOUR OWN TRIBE.
YOU KNOW WE WOULD ALL FOLLOW YOU TO THE ENDS OF THIS EARTH.
PLEASE, DO NOT QUESTION MY LOYALTY AGAIN.
I'M SORRY, ASHTOR. I KNOW YOU HAVE GOOD INTENTIONS...
...BUT THIS TIME THERE CAN BE ONLY DEATH.

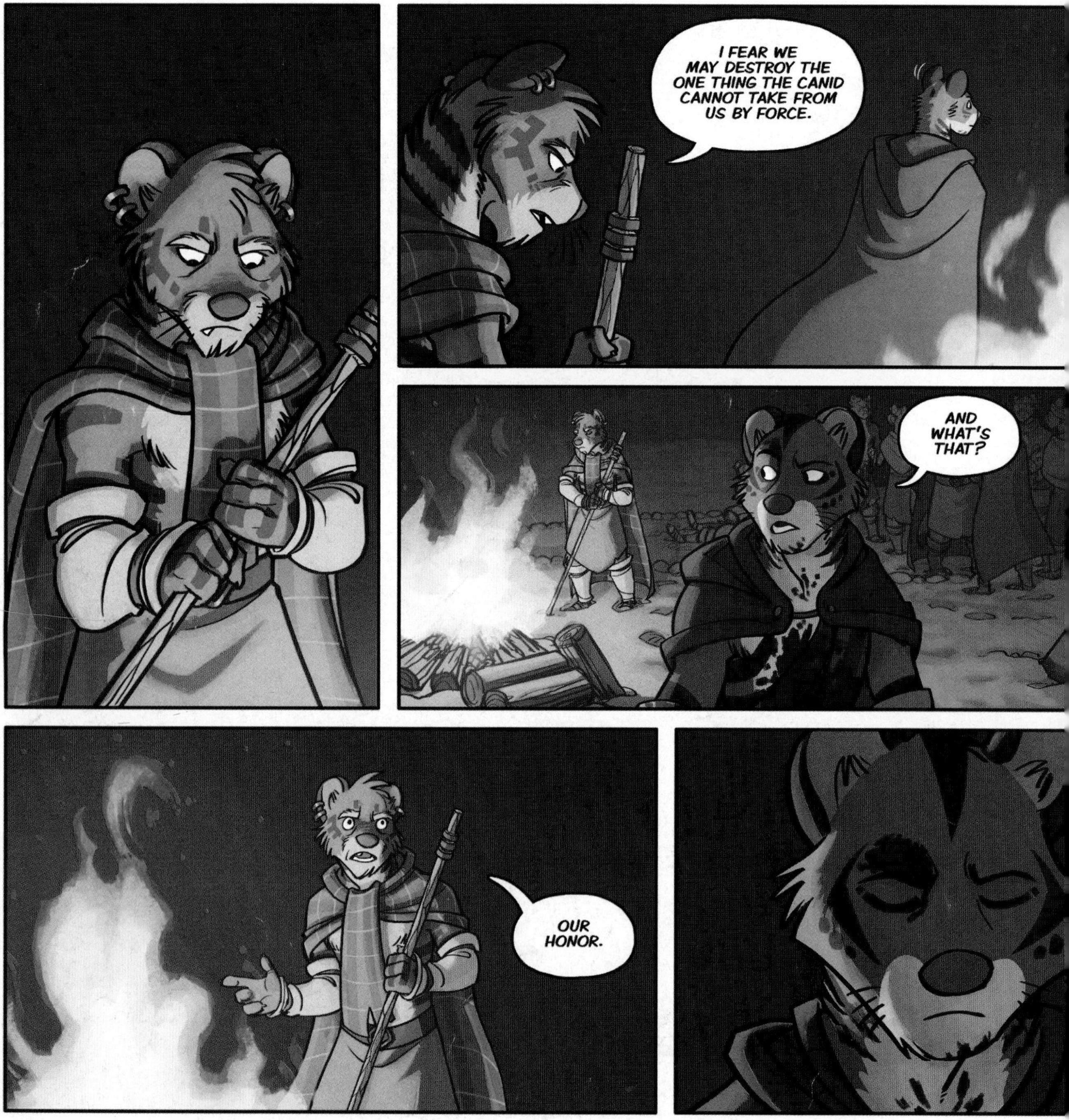
I FEAR WE MAY DESTROY THE ONE THING THE CANID CANNOT TAKE FROM US BY FORCE.
AND WHAT'S THAT?
OUR HONOR.

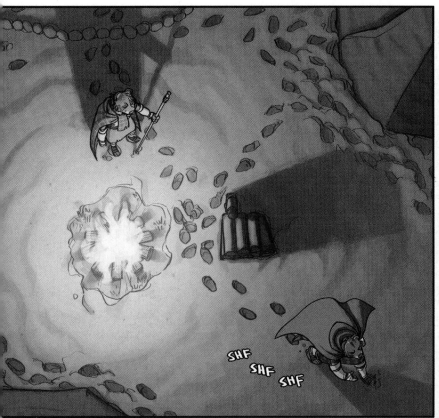

SHF SHF SHF

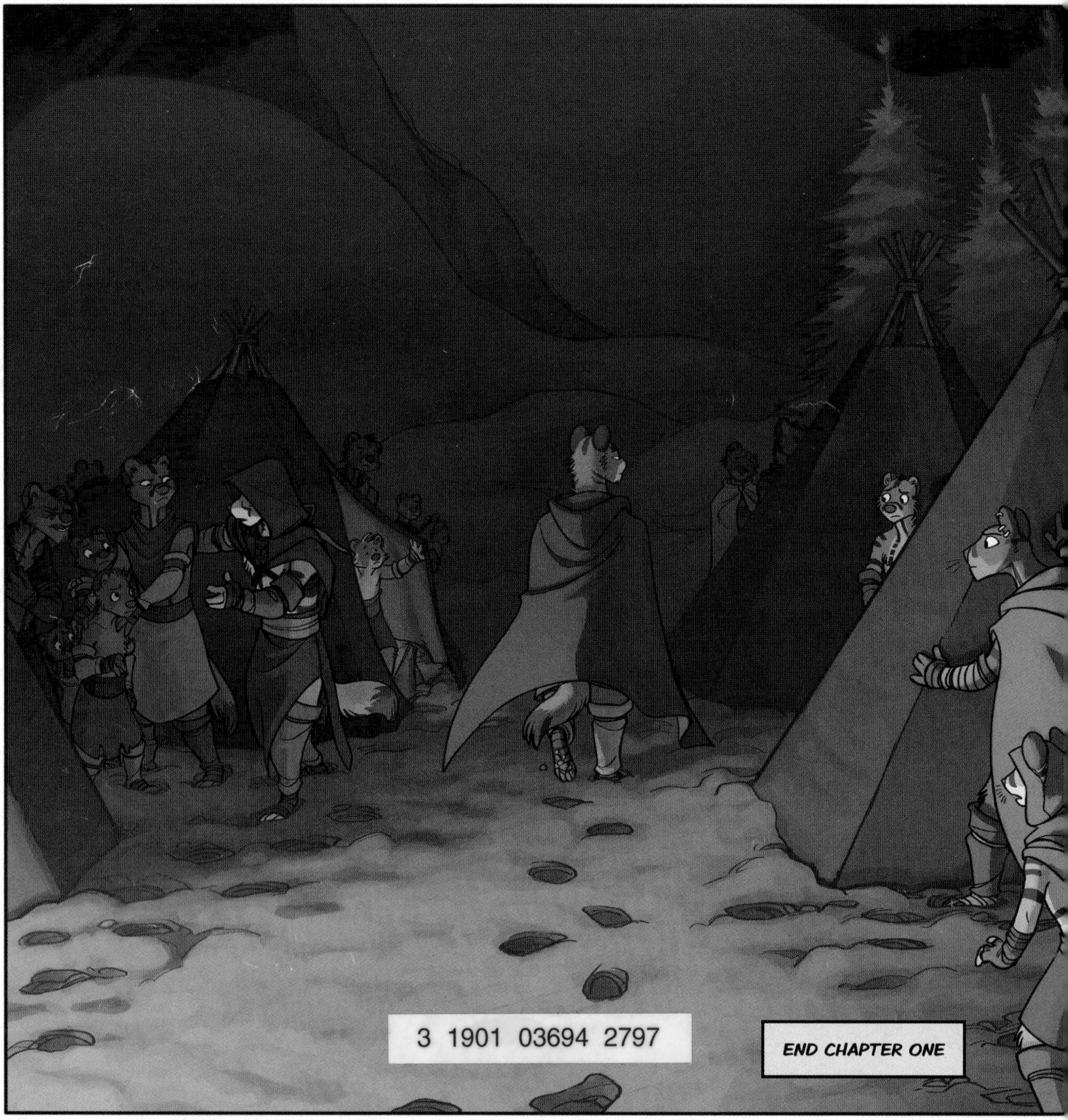
END CHAPTER ONE